Praise for **Sigrene's Bargain with Odin**

"This books shimmers in content, style and power. Zoë Landale, who did her research in Iceland, explores the fascinating world of Valkyries and skyhorses, the world of Odin, Freyja and the Norse gods. Here, shapes and genders shift, horses protect us and trees speak wisdom as Landale tells the heart-stopping story of one young woman's efforts—against the will of two of the most powerful gods—to avenge the rape and murder of her sister-friend.

"The story is told in the form of old Anglo-Saxon verse, in rhythms and images that linger like the pounding of a horse's hooves, long after the book is closed. Here is a book of wisdom—'Who loves the price we pay for anything?' And of adventure—will a mere girl succeed at her self-appointed task before the great warror god Odin, can stop her?

"The tale addresses the question: how do we manage fear and doubt in the face of overwhelming odds? How do we keep our courage and speak truth to the gods? This leads us through breath-taking poems that show how one young woman, still a girl, a mere 'breath-pet,' tries to do exactly that.

"With the beauty and clarity of a fairy tale and the complexity of an ancient Norse legend, we share the tests a hero endures for love of a friend, and of a horse."

—**Kate Braid**, author of *Inward to the Bones*, co-author of *In Fine Form: The Canadian Book of Form Poetry*

"In Zoë Landale's ambitious and remarkable epic poem, *Sigrene's Bargain with Odin*, the reader is immersed, immediately and completely in lyrical legend. Sigrene, half goddess, half mortal, accepts the path destiny commands as she sets out to exact vengeance on the one who killed her childhood friend, Krista, "sister-heart, beloved." Here be skyhorses and dragons, Fire-gods and Valkyries; here a new song animates the ancient legends."

—**Rachel Rose**, former poet Laureate of Vancouver, author of *Notes on Arrival and Departure*

SIGRENE'S BARGAIN WITH ODIN

SIGRENE'S BARGAIN WITH ODIN

ZOË LANDALE

Toronto, Ontario, Canada
www.inanna.ca

The publisher gratefully acknowledges the support of the Canada Council for the Arts and the Ontario Arts Council. The publisher is also grateful for the financial assistance received from the Government of Canada.

Cover design: Peter O'Connor at Bespoke Book Covers

Library and Archives Canada Cataloguing in Publication

Title: Sigrene's bargain with Odin / Zoë Landale.
Names: Landale, Zoë, 1952- author.
Series: Inanna poetry & fiction series.
Description: Series statement: Inanna poetry & fiction | Poems. | Includes bibliographical references.
Identifiers: Canadiana (print) 20230470831 | Canadiana (ebook) 20230470866 | ISBN 9781771339681 (softcover) | ISBN 9781771339704 (PDF) | ISBN 9781771339698 (EPUB)
Classification: LCC PS8573.A5315 S54 2023 | DDC C811/.54—dc23

Printed and bound in Canada

Inanna Publications and Education Inc.
210 Founders College, York University
4700 Keele Street, Toronto, Ontario M3J 1P3 Canada
Telephone: (416) 736-5356   Fax: (416) 736-5765
Email: inanna.publications@inanna.ca Website: www.inanna.ca

This book is dedicated with affection and gratitude to my mother, Barbara Simmins, teacher, lover of words, mythology, and reading. My mother was the kind of person who kept a hefty two-volume Oxford English Dictionary within easy reach so our family would have the definitive answer when, at meal times, we'd argue about the meaning or pronunciation of a word. Mom would leap to her feet and check.

When I was growing up, once a week she'd drive us four kids to the local library where between us all, we borrowed so many books we had to carry them in a two-handled wicker laundry basket, one person per side. This, she taught us, was only right and proper behaviour; you wouldn't want to run out of books.

It's thanks to my mom that I still need a large bag of reading material beside my bedside table in order to feel settled.

CONTENTS

PART 1

IN FREYJA'S HALL

⟨⟩

Summer morning on Asgard's high plateau, so early that sun
sang silver to motes in the air. Dew-damp grasses swiped
cool streaks of wet across my legs and Sleipnir's silver

fetlocks, darkening, drawing them into points. We were playing
Valkyries and heroes when the skyhorse pricked
his ears and a moment later, Loki and a wolf pup

tore around the corner to the bluff looking onto
rainbow spray from the Cloud river far below. Loki was out
in front, laughing. Green-starred clods of moss, offered

to the air, spattered from the puppy's paws. This was Finn.
I'd been told his coat smelled clean as the wind, was fabulously
soft. Prophecies about Ragnarök foretold

he'd do bad things, but even the Valkyries, who exulted
in blood, had kept exact details from me. I hadn't set eyes
on Finn until then. I saw the sweetest face, each

hair grey but black-tipped, with a texture
that made me want to reach out and touch,
see if his coat was as velvet as the Valkyries' tales told.

Finn's ears were too big and his paws the size
of tree rounds. His legs like saplings. I was seized
with joy and wanted to play. I walked straight

up to him—this is how young I was—and
went to hug his neck. He was a baby wolf; I ached
for him to be my friend. Finn knocked me over, and,

black lips wrinkling back from his teeth, darted open
jaws with snake-like speed toward my face. Only
there was a clatter of stones as Sleipnir wheeled, nosed him off.

Finn sailed a dozen feet, landed with a *whump*. This
quick save by Sleipnir from the wolf's snap of gleaming teeth took
away my breath. Blue shock thrilled

through me as I lay there, gasping with the speed
of it. I was no stranger to being hit: my mother, the stinging
clouts of battle-hardened Valkyries, swift

of arm. Before, I believed animals were part of me,
as if they were my hand or foot. It was a serious matter
to have been so wrong. My misjudgement

tattered my world. Finn was brother to the underworld
goddess Hel, to the Jormungand serpent, but I didn't understand,
had seen only the fright in him, his quick cower, and urgency

to make it better hurt my heart. I wanted to
cuddle him. As a child, I didn't know what a toy
was. Maybe I wanted the Doom of Asgard as my toy.

Now, Sleipnir planted himself between us.
I rolled to my feet, blinking. The wolf pup got up
and shook himself, eyes narrowed at the unmistakable

stance of hooves ready to batter. Finn bared his teeth,
growled, *I will remember this, brother*, and turned toward
Loki with the glitter-blue eyes like lapis, who touched

his wolf-son gently on one ear and took him from there
before I had wiped the earth from my hands, still tingling
with fear-spikes. And a sense of life being less than

it had been: scarred, marred, perilous. The glow
that had magicked my world had gone. I felt like grit
in my own eye, as though some round gold

to my days had fallen from the air with Finn's snarl
which I couldn't stop seeing. Dead, who would shed
eye-rain for me? I leaned on dappled Sleipnir,

breathed in his sweet breath and he inhaled mine. We stayed
touching the rest of that echoing day. The next day Odin sent
Finn away from Asgard to a secret spot.

The gods had thought to tame Finn or raise him so
he would be a friend to the Aesir. The attack on me said
that was foolishness. The wolf's destiny and mine linked, spun, set.

My name is Esja. In memory's dark mirror, I stand
before Freyja's hall. Yellow birch boards shine;
spring sun forces my eyes to narrow. Underfoot, stone.

Everyone calls me Sparrow, then laughs when I say, *No
I'm not.* Who wants to be a little brown bird? That's not
fair. Maybe the ship of night will help me win back my name.

The hall rises, a whale to my herring, defining
who I am, Freyja's daughter but only half god. My hair dangles,
tangled, across my eyes. It itches. I dress

myself in the Valkyries' castoff tunics, hacked, fraying.
This one's loose threads tickle my wrists. The linen feels
softer than the scritch of wool, good as a skyhorse's face,

grey Sleipnir who lowers his ear for me to clutch.
Patient as a mother cat with a kitten, he touches
my shoulder with such gentleness Valkyries laugh: so much

scarred warhorse devotion. For them, it's a sign
of something fresh in the world, the sight
of a child and the stallion pausing in sun,

the mismatched pair we are. Our devotion blazes
like a bright shiver of the sky-candle on a blade;
shield-maids are partial to that blink

of light though too wolf-hearted themselves to mother
any. Now the skyhorse tosses his head and mutters;
I lay a brown star-hand on the muzzle known as *Crusher*.

Only in Asgard could a person be four-fathered.
That was me. I didn't find out until one hero, fierce
and mean-spirited, jeered at me and I ran to Freyja

asking if it was true I was half troll. She told me the story then,
combing one of her Gib-cats in the dim stable, her face turned
from me so I saw only the words spill out, sparkling in the

straw-dusty air. No, I had no troll in me. My fathers were clever
kings. Dwarrow kings. Freyja had met them when they came
to see her with a treasure they'd made, Brísingamen.[1] Of course

she wanted the necklace, amber and filagree sun-bright gold.
It seemed to flame in her own great hall and the spell-glamour
of *seithr*, sorcery, beaten into it set up in her a clamour of greed.

I put Brísingamen *around my neck, she said. I could taste*
the power I could summon, wearing it, and I thought
of Ragnarök and how greatly we need every thin

wedge of advantage in that Last Battle. So I said
to Dvalinn, Alfrik, Berling, Grer, who were sweet
and told bad jokes: "How much?" They replied, "Four nights." I said,

"What?" They crossed their arms across their chests.
Grer made it clear: "One night with each of us." The Gib-cat curled
its lip and jumped down from the table. Freyja cleared

her throat, beckoned its brother up to be groomed.
I offered your fathers treasure and jewels. But they insisted, "The gift
of those nights with you." My mother turned to face me, gold

warm as sun at her throat. Freyja clutched her walrus-ivory
comb. *Sparrow, your fathers are kings.* She turned back, intent
on grooming again. *You tell those* einherjar *if any idiot*

is fool enough to call you a troll again, I will
know it and bury that hero in the cesspit for a week—
up to his neck. I walked away, wondering

if I was worth Brísingamen? At least I wasn't a troll.
The skirling wind outside the stable threw
sharp grit into my eyes; I brushed water from them.

Where Bifrost ended, on the Midgard side, the ground
fell down to the river where water hurtled from glaciers,
the torrent unbound now after months of frozen gloom.

Birches peopled the bank, rustled secrets.
I liked to clatter across the bridge and speak
with the biggest, Vinkona. Its prayer made me feel safe.

I'd close my eyes, tuck forehead to rough trunk, worried
this time our exchange mightn't work, I wouldn't
understand. But then in rushed colours and whorls

that twirled, I'd hear the sound of wood singing its life song
to the sky. Sometimes I'd cry; it made me feel so thin-skinned.
Why, I belonged in the world as much as the green scrim

of birch leaves. These round minutes were hard to come by,
more precious than gems set into beaten
silver filagree, winking in firelight. I had no doubt the birch

loved me like sun. How rare it is for any of us to stand
inside our bodies, stand as if the air adores us, as if the sharp
anguish we carry were suddenly gone, while surprised,

we reached out a hand, off-balance without grief's weight.
This tree opened me into rootedness, coaxed the child I was
into laughter, delighted by the damp hug of spring, its welcome.

On bad mornings, I'd ask Vinkona a fortune for the day. Swift
as breath, the birch blessed me with luck runes, sweet
as mountain meltwater booming exaltation to the sky.

At last, to prove my fathers weren't trolls, Freyja let me
visit them in Nidavellir, that sun-bowl in the bare mountains.
I went in fear, wearing what I didn't know were rags. Many

were the gifts my king-fathers gave me, the greatest
that they thought I was wonderful, their girl
where there had been only a cavern in the mountains, grief

in their eyes. For I was their one child, always and only.

Dvalinn, his eyes blue-starred with age blinding, his dwarrow
jokes that I got only sometimes, I was his daughter
and the daughter of all the others. They became dear

to me. Dark Alfrik with his ready smile, his beard longest
of all; Berling who hugged me tight as an ice-bear, who'd lost
part of his tongue in battle so he lisped.

Berling taught me to look at stars. Grer lived for the hot
smell of metal in his forge. Stories said he
could persuade even birds from scrapping; his

talk flowed on, plashing like a river until a person blinked, agreed.
Then he'd smile and twinkle; you realized an
enchantment had smoothed his words until you'd accepted

the sense of them like a cold glass of water and drunk them
down. But it seemed Grer could only use this talent
to make peace so no one took exception. I think

he'd been the one to beguile my mother into her bargain
for Brísingamen. I wanted to stay with my barrel-
chested fathers in Nidavellir's sun-scoured brightness,

their kindness made my eyes seep. Back in Asgard, when
I beseeched Freyja, she pulled out a pocket full of threads, wove
seithr. She said, *Not until the end of days, so say both the warp and weft.*

↕

Krista came when I was six. I saw her size
with a surprise I remember still. I had never seen
another child. The hall tables too tall for me to see

over. Krista was half the height of the *einherjar*, the far-
seeing heroes who hold down the benches, fourteen
to a side, in Freyja's hall. Addý, Krista's mother, foolish

or brave, had a face so scarred she looked like a grim
who'd haunt a lake. A drunk fighter had cut off her lips, ground
them underfoot. Something she'd said. Her teeth showed, gruesome

as a skull. Blink: I saw the girl, the mother, mewing
like a gull, a hand on her daughter's shoulder, meaning,
Behave. The Valkyrie said these others were meant

to look after me. Freyja's orders. *It's time you learned
you aren't a horse.* Krista had a braid neat as a tapestry knot. I leaned
toward her; she looked clear as one of those lucent

brown creeks that flow in high passes. I thought she was tiny
but when we measured back to back, we'd find she was two
fists taller than me. Then I learned a second new thing

in Sessrúmnir with its rows of benches like a boat:
what a child looks like when she feels sorry for you. Boastful,
I said, *Freyja's my mother. Do what I say or I'll send you back to Bifrost.*

Two children lived in the house of the dead,
a hall vast as several whales, a ship upside-down,
yellow-birch-planked, its belly swollen with deaths

to come. Freyja housed half of the clasp of heroes
who'd die at Ragnarök. It was an honour
to be Valkyrie-chosen, picked when the heat

of battle had faded to groans and the hard-feasting
of ravens. Odin's hall, Valhalla, held the other famous
einherjar. My day-star mother had a face

bards sang of and a body men wanted. I looked
nothing like her: short-legged, dark, plain as a lily
stem with no flower. Freyja was goddess of love,

of bare limbs sprawled over one another, succor
of that built-up flash of release, then sticky
peace, if that can be called love. I didn't like shared

hungers, not moist shuddering ones like grease
between the lips. Krista and I kissed to see if it was good.
After, I spat hard to get ease back to my mouth, the grain

taste of her lunch not something I wanted.
Sparrow and *the Thrall's Brat* were what
the heroes called us. Krista and I were

the *einherjar*'s breath-pets, children who lived
while they fought to the death each day, looking
to be at full force for Ragnarök. Their own warm lost

ones long gone. Freyja owned the heroes' lives now.
They wreathed themselves with Valkyries nightly,
glossy-eyed, defrosted with mead. Fate's net

is fine-woven and shines with the hard
far-away gleam of a starfield. In the dim high hall,
the uncle-heroes tickled us, threw us head-high;

we were embossed in the air like gold runes, waving,
or the starfished scrawl as when women weave
magic with wool. Our sweet children's breath warned

them to be gentle. We were the tender living,
Krista and I, set apart from the heroes' lot
of daily death then the painful lift back to life.

⟨

Cloud-lofty Asgard spreads and drifts
a slow, glittering dance of directions,
of power and desire. The god-realm doesn't

play out like figures on a table top. It's not flat.
Asgard is packed worlds within worlds, festive,
massed in an acorn, immense and flickering

through many levels. Rotating? I can say
Asgard had no winter. But I remember seeing
crashing ice-melt on the Heilbrunr river as the season

warmed. I can say: *We knew all the uncles. I can call their
faces to mind.* But while I hold this gold, it turns
into a fish and fins away: god halls were always scooping true

heroes from battlefields, new ones: I helped the Valkyries
with that. Piling the hacked, valiant
corpses into wains was heavy, vile

when I recall it now but at the time familiar; it was
the hot butcher-stink of blood, slack limbs of the warm
dead. I learned to fight on the fields, when

some berserker would charge us. At the back
of my mind, looking forward to a sauna and the birch
smell of the twigs we used to brush

ourselves with in the steam. Then pulling on clean
linen, burying my nose in the tunic, recalling the crisp
snap clothes made drying in the wind from the Cloud

river below Bifrost. Did Sessrúmnir, the great hall
of the slain, slide sideways, out of my hearing
to some other dimension, taking the roistering heroes?

Seasons beat passage over us like skeins of swans,
stitched bright light across the dizzying blue of sky
first north then south, flying shuttles.

My body and Krista's changed from those of children.
We grew breasts. The marks on the cambered
beams by the kitchen, cut by Krista's

mother to mark our height, were as high now
as she was, at least Krista was nearly,
though neither of us would match my goddess mother, not

ever. Freyja glimmered lustrous like the moon. Tall
as a birch, she flickered with that radiance trees
throw like starlight. But even our small breasts troubled

the *einherjar*, the gold-torced heroes we called uncles.
The killing grounds gave them appetites unmatched
by any. In eating, drinking, and in the ugly

sounds, to us, of body fluids shared.
Even from our room, where Addý, Krista's mother, swept
us nightly when the hall's uproar sounded

too threatening, we could hear that. Only we changed.
Not Freyja. Not the *einherjar* who would continue
to resurrect, unaging, until Ragnarök. The Valkyries counted

years but, grown, and half-gods, more slowly than we could see.
Krista's mother had extra white in her hair, but she
was too old, too monstrous with her sliced-off lip slits,

to tempt a hero. Didn't all the uncles love
us? We knew their names, death stories, tales of their lives,
the crinkles of their beards from the time we were little.

But breasts. And Krista way ahead of me as she was mortal
and I, like the Valkyries, half god. The Valkyries must
have read the threads; they made

us ride more to battle with them, insisted we fight so much
Freyja made them back off; Krista was a mass
of slashes and I was lamed for much of a miserable

spring. Were we blind, Krista and I, that we thought
we could play favourites with certain heroes when in truth,
we had transformed from brats into women, and tempting?

Krista's absence in the night woke me. I would
have wallowed in sleep's unknowing warmth
longer but I heard no breath in the windowless

room other than mine. First, annoyance flashed
through me, then I freely admit, the furtive
belly crawl of jealousy. Thorvald was the finest

of all the wound-stick wielders. And
he was Krista's. Brown, his beard shone as
if sun tangled in it, and his eyes aroused

sweet juices in me I hadn't known existed.
But that hero's gaze locked hot on Krista even
though I was the goddess's daughter. I tried to entrap

him with *seithr* Freyja herself had taught me.
The fibres just kept parting though I spent many
hours at the spindle. Finally, my mother

whispered, *The Norns' warp is already*
threaded through the heddles, spin another
working. So I did, created lumpy string out of air,

placed no bounds on the *seithr*. Lack of focus
was my mistake. Unleashing pure fate. Force
beyond my knowing then. The spindle flew

in my hand; I filled it with tangled yarn.
Now, in the dim room I shared with Krista, yesterday's
dun strands of my destiny were yielding

to today's vivid threads, and I breathed out, cross
that Krista was with her lover, while in the close
air, unknowing, I was trapped in a net of blood-red cloth.

Mornings in Asgard started late. The heroes
were in no hurry to die, not after hectic
exploits with mead the night before and the pale honey

of Valkyries' breasts and thighs, the fragrant bush where legs
join to torso. The explosive juices of women. Uncles lingered
at the hall tables, talking, in satiated languor.

None of them knew where Krista was. Even Thorvald.
They'd parted past midnight in a grove they
liked to meet in. Eyes the light brown of leaf litter

looked up from where he sat tearing fish into chunks
with big scarred hands, beard still crusted
with Krista's pleasure. Smiling. A giant's horse had cantered

over Bifrost, alone, and he and fifty others
had gone with Heimdall to see if any oak-
skulled Jotuns needed dispatching. That would be the outcry

at night I now dimly remembering hearing. The roistering
heroes looking for giants. They were always ready
to slip into a killing rage in a good cause. The red

mist that came over them so fury became a blade
that wielded them: they saw only red, the bitter
clang of metal on metal was their delight. Berserkers

they'd been called when they were alive. They were
greatly feared. Fighting, they became something that was
more fire or dragon than human. This time, when

they searched, the *einherjar* found only the mare that Sleipnir
had claimed. So Thorvald said, slurping
hot spiced ale and looking at me with such

tousled maleness I felt my heart squirm.
So where was Krista? Her mother saying
crossly, *I don't know. She thinks she's*

outgrown any responsibilities around here.
And it was true. Krista thought she was half
again as good as any Valkyrie, though hesitant

and slow in battle. She was human, butterfly-vain,
drunk on her own beauty, though it took vexed
years of thinking to outgrow my own vast

grief enough to see this. So it was like her to steal sleep
while in the hall, Addý and I served;
we seethed and plotted sharp words to say.

Krista's mother walked the half hour to Valhalla. I refused
to go with her; I sweat now to remember
the jealous wings of burnt orange rage

that flurried in me. Had Krista found some other lover
more desirable than Thorvald? Had she left
for Valhalla when he'd deserted her for the lavish

joy of bashing in Jotuns' heads, not that there were
any in the end? In wet gullies in the uplands, peepers wheeped
flutters of sound, stilling when a person got close. I wish

now I had gone with Addý over the green
heights, runneled with spring streams, the gracious
light of early evening not yet pinkening and giving

that strange amber radiance that fills the air just before sunset.
Odin's wife met her at Valhalla's massive doors; I see
Frigg's prophetic shine as if I had been there, stooping

to greet the much shorter mortal. Frigg placed both hands
on Addý's arm. *Your daughter lies beside a wild rose, high
as your head. I see turf cut and pulled over her.*

At this, Krista's mother wailed so the air
itself ached and fog whistled in, or so it was said after.
With turf over her, Krista must be dead, not alive.

This was the realm of the gods—rocks would
not rise up to hurt us, the wind rose only while
our backs were to it—malice alone could harm as when

Loki played tricks that only he laughed at, mouth
always with that tense smile, blue eyes malicious
as troll-fire. I hated how his eyes made me

see bones and gnawing. Sometimes my bones, sometimes others'.
But the All-Father had Loki chained now, only
his wife stood by him. Loki hadn't hurt Krista. Only

who had then? Asgard's boisterous heroes came
bursting out into the evening. The search for Krista
began. Some quartered high ground, some called

for Thorvald, last to be see with her. Between blows,
they asked where to find her body. Frigg's prophecy blowing
like a winter wind down everyone's back.

No murder had ever occurred in Asgard before. Odin
said the killing was ill-omened, a sign of Ragnarök's opening
like jaws. The *einherjar* tortured Thorvald. He said only

that he and Krista were lovers. He did not whine,
said he would never harm her, willed
her only good. It must have been the giant whose

black horse they'd found. I watched him
begin to revive, groaning as blood ran up hillocks
to re-enter his severed veins, as flesh knit, teeth hissed

and rooted back into his bloodied mouth. If I died,
I'd remain dead. So would a Valkyrie. Only heroes dispatched
on the killing field came back. Krista would stay dead.

Now, on the killing field, shadows from lit torches leapt
like badly made Jotuns. I was so lonely,
night sharpened into a spear point and leaned

hard on my chest. Looking at Thorvald, I thought,
This is the beard she kissed last night. I thought,
I could have you now. The idea disgusted my thrashing

heart. I squatted uphill from Thorvald's head,
lifted my tunic and pissed, held
back laughter. Looked at the mostly dead hero,

stinking yellow puddled and steamed around his neck.

Three days the uncle-heroes searched for Krista. They found
her, finally, in late afternoon. But the rose bush Frigg
had talked of had been cut down. Only a few finger-size

stems and the roots were left. When her mother
and I arrived, uncles had scooped away the mud
that held her down. Do you know how much

echoing pain a heart can take? The answer is too
much: hearts should explode or tear themselves
into pieces tiny and pale as the thumbnails

of the girl whose hands dragged in soil, whose face
behind the dirt was so blazingly white that you felt
you'd never seen white before, not this final

colour. So you scream, or that's what they say
I did. Krista's mother turned and struck
me on the face. I saw navy sky with moving stars.

The only sound, her harsh panting. *Einherjar*
like stones, planted. Do you know, even
I thought she was accusing me. For envy.

I'd cursed my friend for having what I could not,
for heroes wanting her, for the one I liked never
seeing how my gaze clung to him. He didn't notice

me as anything but a breath-pet. A child
from the living world, a warm chattering
fool who now stood, stricken with the conviction

everyone would think I'd hurt her. But
then Addý hard-hugged me. The breath
she'd been gasping with became

a lament that fluttered like blown cloth in the air
though the floor of the wind's hall was still and all
present were thick-coated with the absence

in that dead face. The laughing girl we knew was gone.
The uncles dug Krista out with great gentleness,
killed in the realm of the gods, what a biting grief,

who could have guessed? *Her braid is gone*, I said stupidly.
Cut off, an uncle said shortly. Her blue overtunic so
ripped it was ruined. Her bare arms slashed.

She died defending herself, I said. Krista's mother
screamed, *Who did this?* fierce as a fox, though any man
there could have killed her in seconds.

In silence, the heroes lifted Krista's body
from the muck, laid her on clean grass. Her legs were bare.
Beneath her were scrunches of clothing, the beige

of her underclothing, her pants. An older uncle stripped
off his cloak, laid down a shield. *We'll put her on this*, he said.
And he tucked his cloak around Krista so sweetly,

I thought, this warrior had a daughter he'll never see again.
Krista's mother screamed, *But this is Asgard!*
How could harm come to my girl here? She waved away

the uncles who had stooped to pick up the shield. *You men,*
she said, and her tone lashed such grief and scorn I saw many
of the harsh heroes flinch. She beckoned to me.

Then, on the shield, its sharp rim hurting our hands, we started
to carry our dead back to Freyja's hall. Sound rose silver
from our throats, desperate sorrow lifted to the softened

blue of sky: Krista murdered, her knife and her braid taken.
She'd been raped, then the rose bush cut off to hide the
grave. Well might Addý motion the men away; one of them

could have killed her daughter. The murderer knew Frigg's prophecy.
In the realm of the gods, where all were allies, who could possibly
have done this? How could we ever be free from this pain?

Freyja herself came to meet us.
Put down the shield. We stopped, understanding
more was coming. She said, *Addý,* and I saw uncles'

eyes shift, like me, surprised the goddess knew
my thrall's name. For I saw from Freyja's face the knock
that was coming. *It's not right that the dead keep*

company with the living in my hall. I saw
Krista's mother step back, the scream
about to stream from her raw mouth, and I sank

to my knees before Freyja: *Please, I ask three blessings.*
Freyja raised a hand; her scorching power dimmed. The bitter
twist to her lips stayed. She said, *Be careful.* I blinked.

One, I ask that we honour Krista with a dragon ship
and fire. Two, it would be a kindness to have her mother sew
her new, brave clothes for the journey. Three, I ask that Addy's life be ceded

to me. This so she would not be killed with a spear
to the ribs, then burned with Krista. Freyja, sparking
with *seithr*, gleamed chill as frost. *Yes,* she said.

The requests I'd made were seemly. Power wisped
like blue dragonflies around Freyja. It was wondrous
magic to prevent Krista turning into an angry ghost wandering

Asgard at night. She had cause for grievance, being
murdered in this realm of the gods. Well, what blessings
I could muster, I'd send her away with, sister-heart, beloved.

↗

We left Asgard in the half-dark. There were
a third of the Valkyries, Krista's mother, me and what
I had not expected, only a wincingly

small handful of uncles. We were mounted
on skyhorses. Odin had said Asgard, midheaven,
was no place to start a soul's journey. Midgard

was. At a certain beach, we'd find what I'd asked
for waiting for us. Only one god, wearing an axe,
rode with us: Heimdall. I had not asked

any gods to come: Krista was a thrall, less to them
than a songbird. And me? I didn't count. Time
had not warmed my mother; Freyja rarely touched

me with anything but a hard hand.
I wondered if Heimdall felt guilty, that he
who could hear one butterfly's giddy heart

from a thousand others, didn't hear the Jotun
most guessed had killed Krista. A giant's horse had jingled
riderless, over Bifrost the night she'd died. A jest?

Freyja had checked; it was an animal, not a hocus. With
no rider, and no Jotun found in all Asgard's wide
and shining realm. A puzzling, weary weaving.

Now, chilled, the skyhorses in skeið, their smooth pace
that ate distance like fire in dry wood, we reached the place
Odin had told us of. The dragon ship had a high, carved prow;

the boat just bigger than a body. We piled it high with wood
that was also stacked by the fish-trail, waiting
for us. By then it was full dark and the waxing

moon rode the sky. Krista's mother lit the boat, not
without glowering at me, for fate's net
was clear to me that day and my third wish said no

to hers. She wanted death and to float
to sea with her daughter. But Freyja
had given me the lit candle of her life, faint

though it guttered now. The boat's wood
caught flame. We pushed it out. The night was
silky cold and so still, the moon whisked white

spokes on its polished surface. Krista's mother
gave a great cry and splashed after it; many
hands pulled her out. The boat crackled. Misery

bit me like a blade but I lifted my head and watched
the flames thrill bright as stallions down a wide
field, leaping into the chill air while

I watched my friend take the whale road
and didn't cry, for wasn't I a goddess's wretched
daughter, who stood, feet on wet sand and regretted

every mean thought and wished it was me
on that boat, for what had I to live for, midway
between dwarrow and god? Then the boat moved

fast, faster as if she'd hoisted sail. She crackled.
Fiery lines flung light-shimmers against the calm
black sea and a tiny quiet came and claimed

me just for a second, while the sea breathed salt
and cold fumed from the water. The smell of smoke
drifted back to us; the uncles beat on their round shields.

I was brought up on the snake's milk
of vengeance. Everyone who tastes it wants more.
When our horses stepped the skyroads home from Midgard,

a moon lighting the perilous air, I brooded revenge.
Krista's mother and I did not talk. Among us rode
her killer. Or not. But in Asgard: the real

shock of the missing, hacked-off rose bush still struck
us both. No wandering giant, as the uncles stupidly
kept repeating, would have known Frigg's saying.

Nor would Heimdall have drowsed through
the breathing of a Jotun on the bridge. He heard the
clicks a moth made searching for a mate. The thrill

of someone trying to cross Bifrost was the bright
banner of his life. He'd heard the horse that bitter
night, chased it. Thorvald had joined in, left Krista behind.

That meant the killer was a god, an uncle, or a Valkyrie.
That large. And me the least of the valiant
in Asgard. The only lower in value

to my mother were servants and thralls.
If a god had killed Krista, it would take trickery
to uncover: I was no reddener of swords, though

I'd learned to defend myself. How could I get by
a god's sword-gleam *seithr* of total shielding? My battle
plan must be cunning as an adder, low and bold.

Krista's neck must have been broken; it dangled
at an angle no neck was made for. If an uncle had done
it, then I'd stand before a fighter so valiant he deserved

to battle at Ragnarök. If a Valkyrie had lost patience with
Krista—without doubt, the airs she'd put on were
infuriating—then I faced one of my teachers who'd

slice me apart a dozen ways before breakfast.
Now, on the skyroads, I heard saddles creak. Wind bit
black through clothes; I thought of snapping mink. Bleak

fury rose in me. The realm of the gods had been dishonoured.
Odin would see that. Or brawling Thor, who took deep
joy in smashing heads with his magic hammer, dwarrow-

forged Mjolnir. The gods would set straight the invisible
harmonies of Asgard. They'd find Krista's murderer, invite
red revenge to roar in, make cleansing their incantation.

Three weeks after Krista's death, Asgard
had closed over her memory like water rushes around
a thrown rock: a ripple expands, then the ache

of the water's wound vanishes. The neat

circles stop. The rock sifts down to nestle
with the muck on the bottom. The surface glints; no

one remembers the arc of the throw. Krista's bright
laugh, the swing of her braid, were less now than the bare
whock whock of ravens overhead. *You been battling*

with Odin about vengeance again? Heimdall asked. I scuffed
my shoe against his stone lintel, smelled
mead over-sweet on his breath. *I'm to stop, he says.*

The Norns have woven the threads. Odin doesn't
care my friend is dead. Heimdall said, *The bright danger*
of a spear slices through skin, pierces deep

into your enemy's guts. If you want Krista avenged, you must be
that spear, Sparrow. None of the gods have the fierce burn
of caring you do. I said, *I can't do seithr, I'm no one's bane*

in batte. I'm not anybody who counts. And I raced
across the Rainbow bridge so the raw
grief that gnawed me wouldn't runnel

down my face in tears. I leaned against Vinkona, the birch.
Forehead to trunk, I asked, *What should I do?* I couldn't begin
to swallow the hook of despair. Above, a bird beat on the bark,
the taps magnified as I stood asking for wisdom,

really listening, eyes closed in the soft morning, waiting
for the day to yield up something other than the scent of water.

For three weeks Krista's mother had sobbed
at me, pleaded for vengeance. Only Thorvald didn't scoff
when I said murder, but I knew his loyalty was skewed.

He too wanted vengeance for Krista, but as *einherjar*,
his blood oath was pledged to the entire
hall of his shield-brothers; he balanced on a sharp blue edge.

The hammering bird stopped, finally. Trees give subtle
guidance in pictures, colours, and the moment of shift
between. I saw only orange whorls. Fear began to slide

bright filaments through me: I was getting nothing. I heard
a chirp, opened my eyes. A furred white and black head
peeked out from behind a clump of birch. Half

a black-ringed eye showed. I swiped a hand under my
wet eyes, knelt. I'd have to come back to Vinkona. I couldn't map
any action from the colour spins I saw. Maybe

my question was outside the birch's knowing. Under
my knees, the ground felt friendly. Could this animal, unlike
anything I'd ever seen, be my tree's answer? The long fur urged
touch; it looked like a walking blanket, double the size of a cat.

I chirped to it. It took half a step forward, then back. I could
see tiny blunt ears, sprays of cream-

coloured whiskers. Its black nose whiffled.
I saw pouchy cheeks, wondered seed-eater? A wild
opulence of tail suggested it climbed. I wished

this blanket-creature with the showy black edges, the ringed
eyes was mine. So I followed it deeper into the birches, right
over the steep bank toward the Cloud river

until the animal skittered up a tree and launched itself, a square
of flying fur, and slower than ash sparked
from a fire, glided fifty feet through the air, silent,

to land on the outstretched arm of a man I had
never seen before. I stopped, skin prickled, horrified.
Had Krista been lured and killed here?

The stranger was tall as Odin, pale, and the thinnest man
I'd ever seen. His legs like stilts. He wore a many-
feathered blue hat; I wondered if was like my mother's

falcon cloak for shape-shifting between Realms. Even
from a distance, I could see this stranger had an ease
to the way he stood, a richness to everything

he wore that argued he was to be reckoned with.
Not a mortal. Not a Jotun with that build. I wondered,
was he from Alfheim? The gauntlet on his arm was

like a falconer's leathers. As I watched, the furry creature
rubbed its face against his chin; the man scratched its ear, called,
Vinkona says words are easier for this. And clear

as anything, the whole birch wood rustled. I had never
told anyone the name the tree had shared with me. Now
I came close to believing, but: *Does Heimdall know your name?*

I asked. The stranger said, *I am Grímur. Shall we walk
to the bridge and ask Heimdall?* I said, *I will
go first*, and the man gave me a half-bow, which

made me feel a fool but I judged it better
to be thought a child than dead. So we walked briskly
apart to where the guardian god stood between

the mist-wreathed arches of the span, waiting.
Of course Heimdall'd heard his name. He stood with
arms folded. *Bringing bad news are you, Grímur?* The way

Heimdall's face flushed, eyes narrowed, meant anger. Grímur said,
Wouldn't you rather be warned than have an enemy spring
on you like a wolf? Heimdall puffed out his breath, sighed.

You Vanir are all the same, winks and nudges, too
subtle for plain speaking. I thought of course, only a Vanir would talk
with trees.[2] Heimdall said, *Grímur's related to you. He's trustworthy.*

I had relatives? The Vanir looked at me sideways with black
eyes, unreadable as water in a well. Heimdall called, *Before*
you go, Grímur, come back and drink with me. I may believe

your warnings. Together, the Vanir and I walked back to
the birches. I asked, *How do you know Vinkona?* Grímur said, *Through*
the World Tree. All trees speak together and to the one Tree

who traces the Realms and holds them in its branches. I said,
I didn't know this, for we in Asgard seldom spoke
of trees. It was more about battle, prophecies, and the sweet

blank ease brought by mead and sleep.
I asked, *How are you my family?* Grímur smiled.
Around his eyes, long years sank rune-scribbles.

We're related like an old apple and a young one, he told me.
He had a noble face, even if he looked like a heron.
On my shoulder, the Vanir's animal sat friendly as a hand's

light touch, Buri was his name. His fur smelled clean
as a bright wind from the mountains felt cool
when I stroked him. He felt light as a bird, cuddling.

Vinkona asked me to warn you, Grímur said. We sat side by side
on the bank, legs dangling over a ten-foot-high scoop
of blue clay that dropped off to the cobbled shore

and restless green slide of the river. Current boils the size of a body
spun downstream. *The trees all talk together.*
Then the World Tree gives us dreams. I protested, *But*

blood gets spilled everywhere in the Nine Worlds,
feeling contrary. *Why is Krista's death so woefully*
different? Grímur said, *This is the realm of the gods. And, what*

you don't seem to understand, this isn't the first death
of a woman. You are dear to the birches. Their days
of light and dark, sap rising like blood and leafy dreams,

mean something to you. So your friend tree told me, Tell
Esja she will be killed next. (The tree knew my real name!) He tickled
his blanket creature so it stretched, touched

his fingers with black needle-tipped claws. Buri lay warm
in my lap. *Who would want to kill me?* While
I protested, underneath the thought slid, white

and pointed as an icicle: two Valkyries had gone missing
in the last few months. They'd been training in the Gap, the great mint-
scented abyss between worlds. Only their skyhorses returned, mucky

with lather and shaking. A willow wand of realization struck
me, hard and thin. Those Valkyries, Talin and Magna, were of a size
with Krista. I could feel the lash of the wand burn my heart. So

truth feels. *Haven't you felt the malice?* Grímur asked now, gently.
His wine-coloured cloak so fine-woven it almost glowed
in the moist rushing air. I whispered, *I thought it was because I wouldn't give*

up about how the gods needed to avenge Krista. The Vanir sighed.
Ask yourself how you can uncover the murderer. The green secrets
trees tell are circles and hard to decipher. I know only that you are not safe.

I am to give you this. He handed me a polished wooden box,
thin, smaller than my palm, the colour of mead, and backed
with silver hinges. Inside, silk wrapped a flake of—yellowed bone?

Bewildered, I looked into Grímur's eyes, the dark of birch where
bark fissures. He said, *It's a shard of Original Sky.* Wonder
shivered through me. *Ymir's skull?* I asked. *What*

do I use it for? Grímur smiled. *I know as much*
as Buri here. This treasure is called Opna. At the moment
of your need, ask the World Tree who links the many-

faceted, lit-up Realms of the living and the dead. The box is made
from the Tree, a branch once struck off by Thor's hammer Mjolnir
when he was after a Fire Giant. The box is dwarrow-made.

Destiny was not something I'd thought to wear
for years. That searing green rolled over others, the wave
of fate so enormous, a person swam along, or, worthless,

tried to duck. I shook water from my eyes, panted
from my fate's weight. Someone had killed pretty
Krista. The birches said I would be next. I preferred

to take action rather than stand like Asgard's magic boar
in his pen, waiting to be slaughtered. *Start with a name,* bright
Grímur had told me, rune-caller, relative. Could I be brave?

I understood I would have to take one wily step after
another. Freyja loved to bet. Who among
us doesn't like to win? I found her with her Gib-cats and

burst out, *Freyja, I want the skull of the one who murdered*
Krista. My mother laughed. *How will you discover this one, mm,*
Sparrow? There was my nickname again, a tiny bird with mud-

coloured feathers. *With* seithr? Taunting. We both knew my spells
were like unreliable shards of iron to her lodestone. I showed
my teeth, said, *Will you bet with me? I'll pull such*

proof from the threads that you agree. Then you
get my cuff Telerion and I get the skull. Freyja's eyes flickered. *The yarn*
must tell such a smooth story there's no disagreement, yes?

Freyja's cloud-deep eyes shone. She had wanted my cuff
from the moment she saw it. The treasure was far too good for a child
who didn't know how to take proper care of anything, she claimed.

Freyja said, *And you must take the skull yourself. Do we have a deal?*
One of her Gib-cats flicked a tufted ear, eyes as green as destiny
in the dim candlelight. I nodded yes to the deal, said, *Why don't*

you ever call me by the name you gave me?
Esja. My name is Esja. And no one ever says it. Maybe
I'm tired of being called "Sparrow." Maybe—

But Freyja was growing taller as I spoke and the ice-wind look
in her eyes scared me. A beating could leave me limp
for days. So I left before I could accuse the goddess of low

cheating, which she was. Uncovering the murderer's name
was one thing. But making it up to me to deal out punishment, no,
that cut our agreement to near worthless. Freyja thought I'd never

succeed. She thought I'd botch the *seithr* and back
down. Fury's dark shame crashed through me, bleak
as one of Thor's thunders. But she'd made the bargain.

Dew still clung to the grass when Sleipnir and I clattered up to
Heimdall's hall. The day's colours were still muted. Truthfully,
my plan was a starved dog that scared me; it loomed, growling trouble.

The Norns lived in Asgard, only a corner that Heimdall
kept off-bounds. A slighter bridge than Bifrost hung
between Urd's Well and the whale-ribbed halls

of the gods. I said to Heimdall, *Freyja said I could go,*
which was not exactly untrue, for I'd said I'd get
the murderer's name through *seithr*. My game

to uncover him before he got me. It wasn't fair that Odin
protected this killer among us. Only
the prickly round of our days was never fair; we walked on

luck. Sometimes it held. Now Heimdall frowned, moved from
the wisp of span he'd been blocking. I was riding fast
Sleipnir. *Odin know you have his horse?* I said, *He's far-*

seeing, isn't he? Feeling spiky, because of course
I hadn't asked. Heimdall yawned, said, *It's common
for Odin to ride out at noon.* His seamed face crinkling.

I'll have Sleipnir back, I lied. I had no idea how far we'd
ride. The bridge, if that's what it could be called, was
see-through. It held the gods, so it should hold our weight.

I looked down only once. Bards call Sleipnir
eight-legged, but he has four, along with a sweeping,
swan-proud idea of his own importance. His speed

is twice that of other wind-racers, truly the air's knife.
*Good luck, Sparrow. No one from Jotunheim killed
your friend*, the guardian god called. Kindness

lit his words. I was surprised, but I shouldn't
have been: in Asgard, the air was porous, stories
swam from our mouths to ears we were sure

weren't there. There were few secrets. Only
I was sure the hero-uncles held back one:
someone knew who'd killed Krista, they just opted

not to say. Probably not Thorvald. One of the Valkyries
had seen her getting dressed after he'd vanished
to join in the hunt for the giant. Her missing knife vexed

me. It said: not a servant, not her mother (I'd wondered).
Though now her mother searched the woven willow
of the *einherjar's* chests for that knife. Weeping.

Well might the guardian god wish me luck. He was angry
that anyone thought an enemy could slip into Asgard
without him hearing. I waved a hand to Heimdall in answer.

PART 2

DOWN PAST THE WORLDS

⟨

The World Tree, Yggdrasil, overhung
the well we had come to find. Other-
worldly calm flowed out, overcame

me as Sleipnir clopped into the glade.
I could see peace, transparent but with a green
sheen like mica, rising in a gold

shaft of sunlight. It greatly
comforted me. We made for the high coping of grey
stone around the well. It was round, a giant

of its kind, big enough for black-beaked swans
to swim in, though surely none would be so
foolish. Then pure *seithr* surged

through us, so bubbly, Sleipnir whinnied.
As we neared the well, *seithr* felt as intense as wading
under a waterfall. I quivered. Where

were these spinners of our life-webs? The World
Tree dripped in glossy welcome with
its nine-fingered ash leaves. Then, beside the well,

the three Norns blinked into sight. These were brushers
of the sky, Jotuns, with colourful robes and burnished
hair, brushed back and pinned into twists. Gold bracelets

circled their arms and their clothing was woven
so finely, a queen would count herself well-
pleased. These Loom-tenders wove destinies: who

would feed an eagle, who would die a straw death.
I quaked. Who was I to stand here and demand
anything from these shuttle-slingers who delivered

luck and ruin to us in coloured wool? The Norns snipped
our lives. And how was it these fearsome sibyls
still had bright hair? They weren't crones as stories said.

I had imagined these doom-dealers were hideous.
We blamed them for everything wrong, hags
who brought death. But I saw now how

lovely their faces were. And surely, that
was kindness in the blue-robed one's owl-tawny
eyes? *I am Urd*, she said. I would have thought

her youngest, but she was also named
What was. Wearing bright russet, the middle Norn
had eyes grey as evening. Numinous

seithr outlined her; like lightning
tamed, playful as an otter pup, it licked
along her arms, nibbled round her hands, long-

fingered. *I am Verdandi*, she said. *What
is now*, I thought. The third Norn, when
I looked again, was still there, but like wax

warm enough to be pliable, her shape changed;
her robe went from violet to red, her clear
skin wrinkled. She said, *I am Skuld*, and came

closer. I knew this Norn to be *What is
becoming*. Staring at Skuld, who pulsed in
and out of different monster forms every few breaths, I

thought, *I'm Sparrow who has flown into a fire.
I will die, shrieking, in these flames. Only Frigg,
who prophesies, will know my fate.*

The Norns invited me to dismount. I slid
from the saddle, legs shaking so
shamefully it was all I could do to stand.

Sleipnir nickered, butted me with his head.
The solid feel of him, hard-
muscled beside me, helped. He wouldn't hesitate

to take steel for me, nor I for him. *There is no record*
of any receiving harm at the Well, I reminded
myself. Red-robed Skuld roared,

blew up into to a troll, deflated to a woman again. *There*
is always a first time, she said. *Here, thoughts*
wheel and turn, bright as shoals of fish. We see them

swim. Verdandi's tunic the dark orange
of hearth-coals. She held out a greeting cup. I took it. Oh,
the fragrance, clean as morning. It opened

my heart, this water with sun and new moon swirled
into it, headier than mead. Blue-robed Urd said,
Do you know what my well contains? Be still,

listen, and the water will teach you:
the dreams of a baby,
the singing of a tree in midwinter,
the love of a house for those it shelters,
the sheen of memory,
the sphere of the seasons,
the long language of stone.

Hesitant, I said, *I thought your well was the past.* Urd said,
*See how leaves drip water into the well? See
how what we do now*—her hand sketched

a flat line in the air—*affects what has come
before?* I drank down the moon, sweet as caramel
made from boiled sap. I couldn't follow her. *I came*

*to see whose life thread you wove in as the killer
of my friend. Your Loom weaves the worlds: you know
everything: the gods come to Urd's Well for knowledge.*

Changeable Skuld, the Norn I most feared, said,
Will you gouge us out an eye, as Odin did? She snickered.
Sleipnir, warm beside me, stamped

a hoof. *Or slice off an ear, as Heimdall did?*
I straightened. *Whatever body part you decide
on, I'll pay. What is it you have already decreed?*

Had I expected to head out again in an hour, triumphant,
minus a finger? *You stayed with us,* Urd told
me. Had she seen it in the Well or was it a tale

woven in the coloured wool of the World Loom?
You sent Sleipnir back to Asgard. I looked
up at the skyhorse's face, eyes fixed on me, body lithe,

dappled, and realized what the Norns
already knew: I needed him more than the night
does the moon. He was my one brightness, the north

star in my life. *And you will tell me I must give
him up?* I asked. *This is your bargain to gain
the killer's name?* Skuld, dressed in red, grinned.

*This is why you stay with us, to find another shape
to what is coming.* And for once, she stayed
as a beautiful woman, though I was sure

all of them were Jotuns. I am a spear sinking
into my own heart, I thought. Verdandi saw
the raven-wings of my horror at parting. She said,

Despair doesn't serve you. Come, let's spin together.
I touched the sunlight of Sleipnir's nose. Took
the Norn's hand of cracked leather. No need to tell

the skyhorse what to do: he understood speech even
though his tongue wasn't formed for it. His element
was air. He sprang into it. I strangled the endearments

I refused to say in front of the Norns. They laughed;
I'd forgotten here, thoughts finned like blue sharks, lingered
visible. When Sleipnir disappeared, he reeled in my light.

Verdandi, the Norn in the russet tunic, taught me to spin.
To do it well. She sat with me, face soft,
watched my fingers tease the silver strand

of *seithr* from the puffy fleece of not-yet-a-thing
she'd handed me. My spindle was nearly full. *I never
thought I could get* seithr *to lie smooth.* The Norn

said, *Maybe you never had real need.* I thought
of Sleipnir's eager face, nodded. I said, *The thought
of losing him chills me like one of those haunts that*

*drift along the skyroads above battles,
the kind that sucks out humans' souls through the back
of their heads. At least I've learned to banish*

them. Verdandi corrected me, said, *You unweave
them.* All day she'd talked about the uses
of choice, how each moment was an unwitting

pearl, rounded, milky-shining, and what connected
each to a necklace of lost beads was the clear
vision of the thread we strung them on. But that part clipped

off or I got swirled into the almost-shapes, almost-
rainbows I saw sparking from Verdandi's arthritic
fingers; they were swollen into lumpy claws, aged

far beyond what her face told, though she spun more
freely than Freyja. Even then, in the water-sweet middle
of that glade, I wondered, how would a mortal

caught up in battle focus on the necklace
of his life to keep it whole? How would a new
baby keep its tiny string of pearls when night

raiders torched the hall? If everyone learned
to spin *seithr*, could mortals at least
shuttle the threads of their lives to lean

away from disasters? Skuld kept drifting
to where we sat at the Well's edge, dipping
her fingers toward the water and dissolving

into one monster after another. When her drool sprayed
my knee, it ate through my tunic, burned skin.
When I turned to Verdandi for protection, she said,

See through it. So I spun, pulled the wholeness
of my skin from the possibilities that twirled, whirled
through my fingers. The angry blisters paled, shrank. Who

would have believed bubbled skin could be made
smooth again? I saw Skuld was pleased as a mother.
She caught the thought, said, *Aren't I your daughter, more*

of what you are becoming? I saw then, sharp
as if she'd clapped her hands, how my fear had shifted
her into a giant toad, a sticky worm, had puffed her up so

I'd felt weak as when Freyja called me *Sparrow.* What if I thought
of comfortable things? Say the guardian, Fire-Dog, the tender
way she leaned against me, the two

of us sitting on the stone steps up to the next Realm?
The Norn nodded, stayed a woman. What a relief!
She mirrored fear, then. Now I would be ready.

My destiny was a green wave. Spinning with Verdandi,
I watched it carry me like the river's vigour
below Bifrost, where the Cloud river boils like the vast

World Serpent thrashing. The first day, the Norns snipped
away my nickname. I breathed through the cut; not so
bad. Then they clipped the silver word that was me, stripped

its threads right off the Loom. The name that had *been*
me, severed between one heartbeat and the next. Hadn't I boasted
to the Norns about what I would give? I was a blank

breath. Pain as stabbing as when my mother walked by me
in Sessrúmnir, again, entwined about some hero. My
heart hurt at how her eyes slid from meeting mine.

That ghost hurt that said as a daughter,
I was a key that opened no door,
a coin so tiny it bought nothing. A dry

ball of dust skittering beneath a table. What do you say
a name is worth, though, when a dead friend screams
for vengeance, insistent as a sooty shearwater?

So I told myself, as the no-name that was Self flicked
light from the surface of Urd's Well across the fronds
of the World Tree and into my spindle. I told this Self, *Focus.*

I said: *I am a splintered blade but I can still stab.*
But I wondered: was I spinning *seithr* or was it spinning
me? Verdandi, *What is now*, hissed, *Yes-s-s-s.*

ᚴ

Night fell like a cut tree, black so dense that crackles
of *seithr* left trails of light in the air, crisp
see-through tails that fizzled and closed

when you focused on one. My eyes felt scratchy.
Someone nudged my hand with a cool cup; stars
reflected from it (in it?) though the sky

was cloudy. Urd's Well, too, sparkled. I drank down
the stars. The water gave me a shiny heart, sweet as a drawing
done by a child, red as a jewel, with no pain to dwell

on. I liked this not-flesh version. The Norns offered
me neither food nor a bed. In darkness, I spun on
in silence. Was I pulling on a dream, or

puffed possibilities that twirled into fine thread?
Wasn't I the child of kings? I could do this.
I would do this for myself and my friend whose name I told

myself would come back. I could see my friend's eyes, red-
rimmed as though she cried and I was not there to rescue
her nor wipe the grave dirt from her mouth. Time melted, ran.

Still spinning, I remembered my fathers' faces, bearded,
brown as the cliff that descends from Bifrost
on the Midgard side. Makers of gold Brísingamen.

My fathers looked sad, profiles as noble as those on coins.
Why was I ashamed? Because dwarrow count
less than gods, because Freyja never calculated a child

into the price she paid for that magnificent filagree
of gold and amber. It was only the necklace Freyja
wanted. Who loves the price we pay for anything? I felt foolish

I'd ever hoped for more. Night's tent enveloped time
as well as space, suffocated stars and tricked
me into believing that spinning *seithr* was a thing

I could do. *Drink*, a Norn's voice ordered. I knew Skuld's deep
tones, raspy as the gravel every dragon
keeps at the back of their throat for digesting.

So I drank more stars and spun until the sun
escaped the Gap and stroked light onto my spindle.
You've done well, Skuld said. She sounded surprised.

⟨

Skuld asked, *Will you give more?* I laid down my
spindle, so full of *seithr* it wouldn't accept a minute's
more gleaming possibilities, opened my hands, meaning,

Anything. As I gestured, the threads reflected light
from the wet grass, skewering me afresh with terrible loneliness
for my friend, dead. My destiny, lithe as a seal, leapt

and tore from my grasp a firelit and happy
future. I would have to sacrifice all my hopes.
Skuld slapped the spindle into my hand.

I followed her. She led me past Urd's Well to another
smaller pool so deep inside the feather-fronds of Yggdrasil that a
person couldn't see the stone coping two paces away.

This is World Eye. Take the seithr *you have spun
and toss it in.* I teased out handful after handful of *seithr.*
It gleamed luminous as my mother's skin, sank

without a bubble. A day and a night's work gone
in five minutes. Oh, it was hard to let that *seithr* go
but for once I had enough sense not to get

in the Norn's way asking why. *Now you may ask one
question*, Skuld said. The water opened.
Something surfaced: a head, bloated, long-dead, only

a head. I could see where the spinal cord poked from
the neck. I swallowed. Bowed. Cursed Skuld for
not warning me. Pale flakes of grave-wax flashed

on one torn cheek, patches of hair, brown living eyes blinking
away water droplets. Mimir smelled of danger and balsam.
You don't look at all like your mother, he began.

I almost laughed, but with gods it's best to remember
that we are less than a shadow, less than a red
catkin on a tree. The head grimaced. *A poet, hey?* I realized

that again, my thoughts had slipped and swum
from my head so others could see
them in the thick *seithr*-charged air, slid

out like the blade I must become. *What's the name
of my friend's murderer?* I left out the honorifics, the nuanced
way I was supposed to speak to a god. I was not

calm, I was furious at being treated like an insect. Mimir
laughed. *You'll never guess.* Something inside me
twanged like a harp string when it lets go. Maybe

even red catkins had dignity. I hissed, *That could
be why I've given away my name. That could
be why I gave your well all that* seithr. *That could—*

Mimir blinked; turned my voice to sand and ash.
Stopped my throat. The god's head said, *You don't amuse
me.* Mimir sounded remote as an ice fjord. *But about*

that name? I nodded. *Tomorrow. Bring more* seithr.
Ask as if dark-maned Sleipnir's life depends on it. The head shook,
sprayed water like a dog, glowered at me, and slowly sank.

Urd companioned with me the third day,
What is past. The Norn touched my arm, a blue-robed daystar
reflecting kindness from the Well's surface. *Don't doubt*

your voice will come back, she said. It did, around
noon. My hands were bleeding by then, cracked and
dry from the slither of *seithr* as I spun. I was frantic as

a brown mountain beck dashing water
thousands of feet down to the ocean; Mimir had warned
me that my skyhorse's life hung on my work—

And your manners, Urd said. *Consider what Mimir
has lost.* Her voice gentle as the breeze fingering the mighty
World Tree, its leaves clacking in what might

have been a language. Urd cocked her head now
and then, as if listening to whatever green news
the divided leaves brought. Water in the nearby

Well smelled sweet. I rubbed my face. *I was a fool—*
Yes, Urd agreed. That was encouraging. *What can I surrender for*
Sleipnir? I said. Sorrow swam across the Norn's face:

Your past. Of course, why had I asked? *It's yours,*
I said, opening my hands, the spindle trailing the yarn
like glinting spider silk across my yesterdays,

the plum velvet of them fetlock-deep on the grey stallion
who was not in fact mine, only a battered skyhorse
I loved better than any creature under the sun.

To say losing my past hurt is like saying a star's
core is slightly warm. I screamed with the ripping of it, sure
I could feel flesh sloughing off, crackling like a shaken-

out cloak—which Urd mercifully took and folded
away, a shadow-skin. Then I was myself again, feeling
raw, though no longer in pain. *Look at your face,*

the Norn said. I bent over the waist-high coping,
sucked in breath like sea water, cold
and salt-shocking to the lungs. My fathers had given me clear

brown skin: my dwarrow blood was plain. One flick of the eyes
could see that. Only now, my birthright wasn't even
there. I'd become a monster with skin so eerie

it raised goosebumps just looking. In my reflection,
my skin shone silver as a shell's inside, a reckless
swirl of green, blue the colour of ocean reaching

to the sky on a sunny day, featherings of sunrise pink. One
glimpse of me would make a mortal ward off
evil with two crossed fingers. I looked like no creature in

any Realm. I held up my hands. Yes, they were that
strange sea-shell glow as well, only brighter. My arms, the
short legs I pulled up my tunic to inspect. I thought

of Urd folding the unseen skin of who I'd been before, away.
Will I glow in darkness? I asked.
The moon will love you like a pearl, Urd assured

me. *It will burnish you.* I wanted to howl
like a wolf at the sky, but I'd been asked, hadn't
I? And generous as a god, I'd opened my hands.

〈〉

Before I left Urd's Well, Skuld—*Aren't I your daughter,*
more of what you are becoming?—took me to the deep
water hush where the World Loom dreamed

real ice-mountains and clouds, the slow hearts of newts.
The Loom stood taller than Grímur. I saw it as a noble-
timbered gate trying to pull me through, near

enough to lure touch. The warp and weft were all colours, the
brave love of them; blue, orange, indigo singing together
in harmony that made me weep for pain and twinging

joy. Sleipnir walked there, tiny. I saw then how I could
re-weave that bit of tapestry where death clipped
his lines from mine. Skuld showed me, held out one arm, cautious,

to keep me from touching. *Yes,* I said, bending forward. *A favour*
for Odin. Skuld sighed. *In all Asgard, Tyr the warlord is Odin's favourite.*
For all that Tyr's god-Aspect was so fearsome,

in Asgard we liked him. Tyr was kind as the spring sun,
a great red-cheeked god. I'd watched how everyone straightened
after talking with Tyr, walked away taller, smiling, feeling somehow

more than. And then, staring at the Loom, I started to fall
into it; I saw the terrible thing I was saying yes to. Fear
crackled blue through me, I tried to speak, failed,

toppled. Skuld caught me before I hit the threads. She said, *You
have woven and you have wept and more still will you
give. But go with our blessing,³ and, young*

one, know when the time comes, you will not be found wanting.
Then the Norns sent me off with a stirrup cup and a wailing
in my bones that faded as I forgot what waited.

I recognize the sound of your breath, the guardian god said, snicked
away his sword. *But what happened to your face?* I shrugged: *Same
as your ear.* Heimdall's cheeks blazed ruddy as sunrise,

You're on fire with the murderer's name, aren't you? I whispered
what I'd learned about the horse; he whistled
up a Grey Messenger to check for us. One hand whacked

my knee. *Good work, girl.* I discovered Freyja
in the stables. At the sight of me, she stepped back, frowned.
Her wounding so familiar, all it found

to lash was red scars raised like half-snakes. *Yes. I paid the Norns.*
One Gib-cat showed me its teeth. My mother nodded.
She shooed the beast away, patted a bale of straw. *Your name.*

Your colour. Something else I can't yet see. I sat
and she settled beside me, so close I could smell her skin,
musk and the long slow dream of moonflowers. *Your spindle?*

I unwrapped the rowan wand. My mother sucked
in a breath at the thrumming of power, the *seithr.*
I felt a froth of pride in my spinning fizz up. She'd

been convinced I couldn't master thread. Together we
bent, a mismatched pair, over the weavings.
Together we saw Krista's throat slit by someone we'd

both trusted. The *seithr* looped and wove and
eventually my spindle was bare. Freyja sighed. *It's clear.* As
I unclasped the greatest gift my fathers ever gave me, a

voice said, *Not so fast.* I looked up from the amber and gold
of the cuff Telerion. Odin towered over us, glowering.
This man, your commander, is one of our greatest

fighters in the Last Battle. The two
of you don't get to giggle and trade
his head away like a gold torc or a toy.

ᛋ

Odin insisted on the trial. My mother made that
clear to me. Her fury the size of a waterspout, one of those
grey funnels of two hundred feet known to

suck in mariners and their boats. I have seen them skitter
across the ocean with a deadly shining beauty, so
fast and unpredictable it almost stopped

my heart with wanting to see more closely.
As thanks for the name, Freyja let me keep my amber cuff.
If it had been up to her, she would have cleaved

off Anfinn's head herself and handed it to me, dripping.
Certainly I wouldn't have been one to dip
a blade in his blood; he handled a sword with the devotion

of ravenous flame to tinder. What mattered to Freyja was betrayal;
I'd seen my mother with her commander earlier on the bleak
night he'd murdered my friend. He'd left a goddess to break

the neck of a thrall after he'd raped her. A dirty mortal, a foolish
girl in Freyja's view. But the trial was fair; I forced
myself to hold my head up as though the wind flowed

around me on the skyroads. Loathing him, I sat
across from Anfinn. He watched me with a half-smile,
secretive, intent: *Wait. You too, I'll see*

some dark night when you least expect me. Not
that it was desire I saw in his eyes, blue as ice near
a berg's edge, it was sheer predator necessity

to bring down a heavy paw on his prey's spine, then rend
because he could. Anfinn was blond, tall as a half Jotun. A ragged
scar wormed white across his left cheek. His nose resembled

a sea-eagle's beak. At the end of the table, Odin loomed
over the trial, the force of him so strong, I couldn't look.
Air shivered. One of the sharp-beaked ravens on his shoulder, left,

shit on the floor, flapped back. Hugin and Munin
they were called, Memory and Thought.
They told Odin secrets from all over the Realms, matters

he needed to know. I wondered if the All-Father foresaw
that the murderer meant to kill me too. Was I just flotsam?
Ragnarök was all that counted. He must take me for a fool.

Beside me, Freyja fiddled some threads
in her hand; the murderer's head snapped back as though
he'd been shoved. Odin's voice rang out, *Anfinn, is it true*

you killed outside of Folkvangr? The blond warrior bowed
his head. *Yes.* Surprise mantled up in me the way a falcon bates
on the handler's fist. I thought we'd have to bring

him to this the way wolfhounds chase after a stag,
hard and harrying every twist. In a bored voice, he said, *I am sorry*
for bringing death to Asgard. Not for killing my sweet

friend, but dishonouring the realm of the gods. I glared at
Anfinn. He opened his mouth, laughed, silent, in my face and
Freyja rapped my knee. *Before we discuss wergild, what about*

the story. What did this girl do? And you? The
murderer sat back and told us details so thorough
I had to clap a hand over my mouth to hold back the

vomit. Freyja snorted. *So the thrall said no and you took offence.*
Did you plan this? Anfinn's face mottled at her scorn. *Only*
at the moment, he said. Freyja looked to Odin,

who nodded. He'd forced a trial but this was the goddess's
own hall and her own commander. *Bring in the Grey*
Messenger, Freyja said. Heimdall came in with his ghastly

creature. Fog spiders with beaks, Grey Messengers
were kenneled by Bifrost. *That horse the other night*, my
mother said. *On the bridge. Where did it come from, nine-mothered*

Heimdall? He blushed, twisted his hands. *Jotunheim.*
Brought here by a Jotun. The Grey Messenger jostled
his leg; the guardian god said, *Tell.* The Messenger jumped

to its feet—they clicked—and replayed a Jotun's rumble, *A mortal*
bought the horse. He told me to come at midnight
to Bifrost and that he'd take the horse from me.

Heimdall guided the Grey Messenger through
the Jotun's flat description of the purchaser, there
was no one in the room who could doubt it was the

big-nosed scarred *einherjar* who had just confessed how
he had raped and killed Krista, for I could recall her
name now, though I had lost mine for good in the heat

of working *seithr* at Urd's Well. I said, *You lied*
to the All-Father. Anfinn licked his lips.
You planned this a month ago, it was that long

since your trip to Jotunheim. What did you tell
everyone? I had never spoken as an adult before these
great gods; they had taken on their Aspects. The air trembled

with the crackling immense power of who they were.
Older than mountains, harder than rock, even I who
thought I knew my mother and Odin, wished

this moment was over, yearned to go back to something other
than insect-tiny, frail as a bug in a room full of boots, only
Krista's death still needed avenging. She was the one

I risked this for. Recovering, the commander winked at me.
No. It wasn't me. My job is to train for Ragnarök. My
mother, dangerous as a single enormous wave moving

fast across the ocean's surface, said, *And
was this the first time you killed a woman about
your pleasure?* Anfinn placed a scarred hand above

his heart and said, *I swear by Odin himself.*
A lie, Freyja said, her voice heavy
with the threat of tonnes of seawater heaving.

A Valkyrie strode in, hefting a big sea-grass chest.
This is yours, the goddess said. Anfinn sniffed. *Could
be anyone's.* Odin stirred. The Valkyrie's jaw clenched.

She began to unload the chest. Undertunics. Trousers.
All rich soft fabrics. A whetstone. A cloak shot through
with thread that glimmered blue. A cloak pin and three

. . . hanks of hair. A brown braid, Krista's, as well as others,
blonde. *This is my sister's,* the Valkyrie hissed, one
braid held up. *I gave her this hair-clasp.* Freyja grasped another—

The missing Valkyries. How deadly Ginnungagap
took them. Except it was you, the commander I gave
honour and my trust to. Anfinn blinked, grew

red then pale. *I never saw these before,* he said.
At Freyja's rap on the table, a blonde Valkyrie slid
sideways through the door. I recognized Berglín, she

was the captain, compact and graceful
as a peregrine falcon plummeting on a rabbit, grinning
as she killed. Berglín was grinning now. *Well, good*

try, commander. But Freyja perched me in the rafters
of your room as an ant and— A minute later, I rushed
outside, threw up. After, I stood, panting, by the great red

door of Sessrúmnir. I couldn't go back in. No
more details. He'd killed even Valkyries, no
denying those sad braids, what he'd done over them, no

more, surely that man had ruined himself, lied to the gods,
murdered even Freyja's own fighters. But grim
strands of *seithr* had shown me the trial's outcome. The only good

I could wrest from this was honour. I yearned for a belief
in something clean to power me through this hour; a bright
subtle meaning to the world's weaving. Surely I believed

in the formidable beauty of this pattern after seeing
the Norns' labor, and feeling the deep peace of the sunlit
thoughts that swam by the World Tree. Surely?

〈〉

Anfinn was guilty. Guilty of lying to the gods,
of taking great Odin's name and grinding
it under the heel of his boot. Killing the girl

who had been my sister-friend was almost incidental,
though the deaths of the Valkyries caused even ice-
eyed Odin to blink. The dishonour to Freyja weighed heavy in

the balance. But the goddess was not to have
Anfinn's head: she'd asked. No, the murderer had
that pleasure. He walked from the room free-hearted.

The former commander was too skilled for Odin to sacrifice—
that's how the All-Father put it. At Ragnarök, Anfinn could spin
the tide of battle in the gods' favour, or so far-seeing

Odin claimed. Anfinn walked out of the room, whistling,
as Odin's warrior. *Seithr* had shown me this would
happen, so why did I feel like a spear of white

ice drove itself into my chest when Heimdall sidled up
and told me? I'd stayed outside Sessrúmnir's great door, unable
to go in or move away. *Your friend is under*

the long horizon, the guardian god said. He meant to be
kind, I knew. *Make the wergild count.* Heimdall blurted
this out, blotchy-faced, while I ducked behind

a pillar to get away from his Grey Messenger, leashed,
beak clacking. Oh, I will, I told him. At which long
moment, I heard the All-Father's voice, loud

as a glacier calving: *What wergild would you have
me pay?* I whirled, looked up into Odin's eye, heavy
with a whole moving galaxy, swallowed, said, *A high*

*price. I had two friends in the world. That is
now down to one. And you saw your man, I
wiped my nose, will not let me live long if*

*I stay in Asgard. So I will leave. I have no mind
to be raped and killed as well. My sister-friend wanders the meadows
of the heavens above us. I will go to Midgard.*

*The wergild I ask from you is my other friend,
Sleipnir.* So close, Odin smelled like the brilliant fire
of lightning. *Impossible. It is written, "the fine*

steed" I ride in the Last Battle is Sleipnir. *Ask
for something I can grant.* I slipped on my courage as
a warrior does when she pulls the delicious weight of a

sword into her fighting hand. *It is also written that
you*—I lowered my voice—*will die in your fight with the
Wolf. It is not written that your horse dies as well. Therefore*

*I ask that after you fall, All-Father, I take Sleipnir
from battle.* Odin skewered me with his gaze. I saw
he understood my whole design. Over his face, sorrow

slid dark as when a raincloud slips over the sun but
I saw his mouth narrow in anger. *Because
of your daring, Freyja's daughter, your blunt*

*words are forgiven. But how will
you see me fall and save Sleipnir? Won't
you be fighting with the Aesir to save the world we*

know? I glared at Odin, all discretion forgotten. *Not
now, not ever*—Two black shapes *thwocked* by my face. Now
each ear zinged with pain's lightning. The ravens had notched

my ears. I raised my hands to touch;
they runneled with blood. Shock shuddered through
me. The birds had saved me from further railing that

Odin would have had to kill me for. I bowed.
It's also written, I said, *after the Last Battle,*
a new green world will emerge. With your blessing,

I will take Sleipnir through. Dark as doubt, the ravens
scissored back in the shaken air, landed on Odin's right
and left shoulders. He was going to deny me, I realized,

his Aspect bleak as grey ocean
with storm winds slicing white wave tops off,
sword-cut clean, the crashes of water falling over

blown spume; wind wailing like the end of the world.
Then a flash of red. A raspy Norn's voice I knew well
said, *It is written that this woman,*

Sigrene, for this is the name she drank down with
the stars when she thirsted at Urd's Well, will
not fight with the gods at the last. Willing

she wove, and willing she wept and gave. Her anguish
and her work for this great-hearted horse, was able
to change a few threads, just a few. And

so it is written, the Norn in red said,
that Sigrene will come for Sleipnir who will be sorely
wounded and none knows if she will succeed—

Odin growled like Garm, the black dog that guards
the gates of Hel. He shouted, *No. Sleipnir is my horse and goes
with me, even into death.* Odin was so angry he glowed.

Singed, I spun that night on a spit of dreadful
dreams where I charred and endured. I woke, dazed,
to Krista's mother shaking me, *Sleipnir demands*

you get up. Her disfigured face quivering and wan.
With fear for me, I realized. I could hear whinnying
even from my room. It comforted me after the while

I'd been transfixed, rotating in thunderous black, all meaning bled
from my life. I struggled to one elbow, then went to bounce
to my feet, only to have Krista's mother catch my elbow and buoy

me up. Reeling, I staggered to the outside door
where my dappled Sleipnir waited. Until that day
I hadn't known skyhorses could cry. I buried my head in his dear

shoulder and clung to him. I kissed his nose. Those
tracks of moisture gave me back colour and hope. This
great-hearted horse loved me as the sun loves the World Tree.

The *seithr* had shown me truly: we belonged to one
another. I would **bring this into being**,[4] Odin
or no. I planted myself in the immensity of

this rightness, thrust up and out like Yggdrasil, telling
of green going on forever. Slowly, as I breathed in the tiny
tickle of horse hair, dimensions slid back. Two of us, together.

The singeing had been a patch of my hair as it caught
fire from Odin's lightning. So Berglín, captain
of the Valkyries, told me. She wanted it clear

I was now as safe in Freyja's hall as a drop of water
scrabbling on a hot iron pan. *Coward*, Berglín whispered,
venomous as a viper. *Leave us to do all the work*

of saving the worlds, would you? Too good for fighting?
She spat on the floor. Only Addý's arrival with broth forced
the knife in her hand to disappear. *None of us will forget,*

she hissed and strode out, boot heels smacking the
floor like a *seithkona*'s drum: *dum, dum,* this
way to the Realms muddling, Krista's ghost sifting through

bare wood walls. I touched my forehead. A handful
of charred hair came off. *Why I am alive?* Addý hesitated.
Wiped spit from her lipless mouth with a clean handkerchief.

Well, Odin had to kill Sleipnir and have nothing
to ride at the Last Battle or let you live. It was a near
thing, she said at last. Krista's ghost, nestled

on my wall, blurred with my tears. *Sleipnir. It wasn't a dream?* I heard
the *seithkona's* drum like blood racketing in my ears. Addý held
out the steaming broth. *Your skyhorse came with a great shackle on one hoof*

she said. *Yanked up.* I told her, *Odin foreknew the wergild*
I'd ask for. The drum beat louder. The world
wouldn't catch. From my wall, Krista's ghost waved

goodbye and spun off like blown cloud. I knew I wouldn't see
her again until I killed her murderer. Then, like a storm surge,
an idea crashed over me how to exact vengeance for my sister.

Anfinn, my friend's murderer, was a berserker
in battle. With red-eye rage, he had broken
swords and slain more heroes than any other brave

fighter on Freyja's killing field. This was the man
who would come for me in the night, or as I made
my way alone in Asgard. Unless I could make

him believe I was harmless and dispose of him first.
I liked that word *dispose*, it sounded like taking out fishy
slops to the magic boar we ate daily. *Dinner*, I fondly

called the boar. I could not kill Anfinn. But I would
persuade others. Heroes fawned on Anfinn the way
wolfhounds do on the kennel master. But his weakness was

Anfinn was new to Odin's company of champions.
Their North Star was Fell Fork-Beard, their own commander.
It was his bright praise Odin's warriors craved.

What if their commander was threatened?
Addý could plant rumours; servants spread the
news with the same avid cruelty that

ravens pecked out the eyes of poor
lambs. Anfinn's only ally in Valhalla was powerful
Odin. Truly the full-formed plan

that, like a wave, smacked me from my feet with its daring
must have come from Mimir. The scheme smelled like dawn
and *seithr*. It made me think perhaps I was after all, a daughter

of the World Tree, not the goddess of love. I felt heartened
and half mad. Odin would not let me live if I hijacked
his will. Well, the sun sets for all of us sometime, how

could I fear death knowing Fire-dog, the guardian, would
greet me on the high stairs of Asgard? Her tail would *whish*
in delight. Only my skyhorse would mourn me. I despised weakness

in others; it was time to prove I was worthy. That morning
I asked Addý to spy for me; who better than my murdered
friend's mother? And I strolled past the multitudes

shouting and hacking in Odin's killing field,
beside the vaulting hall of Valhalla, not far
from where grey-maned Sleipnir was stabled. I found

him in a field with the mares and whispered the plan
to him. He blinked lashes long as daisy petals,
shuddered, snorted so loudly I jumped at his plea

for me to change my mind. *You don't have to like it,*
I said. *Just get them to help. Including
these drinkers of the wind to protect me isn't*

something the murderer will expect. We both knew
that Odin would lay claim to his stallion. Sure as a key
turns in a lock, for four days, Odin rode keen-

eyed Sleipnir everywhere. But I went nowhere alone.
A cloud of mares and colts drifted with me and
we walked by the killing field until the brave

warriors didn't even notice me as they fought. I groomed
the skyhorses, picked stones from their gleaming
hooves and watched the battles. Only Anfinn glowered

at me; I shrank as if frightened. I was a weasel.
Addý brought me food. I fed her the gossip I wanted
Fell Fork-Beard to hear, that Anfinn boasted he was

a better fighter than Odin's commander. Certainly he was much
bigger, though Fork-Beard had his measure;
he knew how to deal with rivalry. By the third day's melee

Anfinn went from being one of the last fighters standing
to being cut down in the first quarter hour. I could see
the reason: five heroes, working as a unit, scythed

him down. It wasn't one on one. It was butchery.
Addý relayed to me—servants' gossip—that the brutal
takedown of Anfinn's strutting was popular. It became

a good joke. Fell Fork-Beard had it right:
this was the way to treat a man whose twisted rage
and stealth made him kill even Valkyries, those righteous

shield-maids, arctic in battle. They, like *einjerhar*,
slipped between fighting, groin-grasping, and quaffing entire
heady horns of mead. On the fourth day, early,

the skyhorses and I slipped out to the killing fields. I watched
Anfinn die early again and marked where he lay. Then we
idled away the hours though my pulse was hot; destiny writhed

alive in my veins. By late afternoon, there were three
knots of two fighters left each. They battled at the far end of the
field. I crouched to the level of a skyhorse's back, asked two

mares to walk between me and the *einherjar*. And we moved on
to the killing field. This one and Freyja's were the only
places in Asgard that a fighter could resurrect. No others.

Then, even for a hero or a Valkyrie, dead would be dead.
The field felt jingly with *seithr*. The mares danced;
I felt *seithr* pull through my feet. The mares dithered

when I motioned *forward*. But they moved at last. We picked
our way through the dead. Torsos bore terrible wounds. *I am proud
of you*, I told the mares. They had their ears back. The punch

of slaughter-reek, slack limbs; the skyhorses didn't want to step
on anyone or slither. I found Anfinn; his throat had been slit.
As I watched, a breeze lifted a strand of his hair. He'd been struck

down early, so he'd be among the first to resurrect. I wouldn't want
to have left this much longer. The warriors in the far field were
down to two groups. I drew Krista's boot knife. This was

for her. First, in vengeance, I lopped off Anfinn's *reðri*. Then
his *bǫllr*. I wound his dirty hair onto my left hand, tilted
his head and hacked at his neck. It took longer to sever than

I'd counted on. The last two heroes shouted.
I raised my head; they'd seen me and were coming, sliding
on bodies. *Thank you*, I said to the skyhorses. And the sweet-

faced mare, who I knew Sleipnir preferred, led me to the edge
of the field and a rock. I wiped my knife on Anfinn's eyebrows.
The mare whickered; the heroes were eager

to catch us. I slipped the clean blade into my
boot-sheath, threw Anfinn's bits into a bag and mounted.
Previously I'd only see skyhorses mince

their way up the air currents; this mare bolted up
so fast I started to slide off. We had no saddle. I understood
her haste when a spear *whooshed* by, grazed the under-

side of my foot. I leaned up to her neck and clutched on
to her mane. My destiny was trumpeting like a swan, we'd only
just made it up into the sweet air. *Beautiful one,*

I told the mare. Had the spear edge slit her foreleg?
I slid further back; there was nothing to keep me from
falling. I grasped the mare's coarse mane with ferocity,

lay as best I could over her neck, tried to wrap
my arms around it; they wouldn't reach. I wound
my hands tighter into her mane; it must hurt. The wretched

bag made it harder, my hands shook, but I would not let go.
How long could I hold on? Mane-hair got up my nose then gradually
the mare levelled off. I scrooched forward, sat up, grinned.

Few of the uncle-heroes rode skyhorses. Only
the gods, Valkyries, and me. So we had one
slice of time to *schipp* like a throwing knife onto

the high mist-shrouded span of the Rainbow
bridge; the air would bear us only to the rim
where the wind met stones and sighed, releasing

us gently. I was startled to see the second mare but why not,
she was guilty of helping me, her will
glinting in what looked like a wink

from one dark eye. Heimdall hailed us.
I watched his gaze take in no saddle, the unmistakable
drip of red from my sack, then I realized the ugly

wet feel on my breast was blood too.
And on my mare—The guardian god's sword, a shining tree,
barred our way. This was the charred unknown in the

weaving that *seithr* had not shown me.
Want to see what I have? I asked. *My mother
asked for this.* Heimdall nodded. My

hands clumsy as a tern's claws, I opened the sack,
tilted it to show Anfinn's head, the snarl
that pulled lips back from yellowed teeth. Heimdall smiled.

His sword sang deep as he sheathed it. *It's best
you're away from here before Odin gets back
from Urd's Well.* So much said in the resonant blank

of what Heimdall left dangling, a wish
for luck and, *Avoid Urd's Well. Asgard is in no danger from what
you've done. Since Freyja asked for this: good work.*

Heimdall's tone was warm enough to lean on, a momentary
surprise like a stone wall heated by sun, a most
welcome respite because now came the part that made me

hard-sweat: I had to destroy Anfinn's body-
parts in such a way the All-Father could never begin
to retrieve them. Anfinn's torso might be by

now stirring on the killing field. His neck
stump would heal. His groin would knit
though he'd piss like a woman from now

on. I said to the mares, *Would you go*
with me further? Ginnungagap
is full of dangers. The mare I rode was great-

souled; she answered by stepping up into
the whistling mint-sweet air of the immense
void of the Gap. The second mare hesitated, and turning, I

saw her wheel back onto the bridge. *Worthy*
and brave one, I said to my mount. *You're a wonderful*
mate for Sleipnir. We're going down past the worlds.

The mare and I stroked through air around World Tree like
fish circling a giant rooted kelp. On one side, green leaves
glittered. On the other, Ginnungagap yawned. We descended levels

in spirals, me holding to the *seithr* of **down and
down**, for it was not just the World trunk we moved around,
the massive rustling life of the Tree, but absolute

potential. We bumped down a back eddy of sliding air. If
I hadn't had a lifetime of riding bareback, I
would have bounced over the mare's pale neck into

the endless chill of the black abyss beneath us.
We all used high saddles, the Valkyries, Odin, me, underneath
us when we stepped between Realms. I kept the sack jammed up

against my front. It began to twitch. The mare felt it too;
she laid her ears flat. By the high stairs of Asgard, that
cursed head was coming to life. Right now, the torso

might have staggered upright on the killing field. One
hand might touch its empty groin. If I let the sack go, Odin
might be able to draw it back, even from the depths of

nothingness. Then I felt a squirm like a puppy and
almost let the bag go. The head wasn't the only appendage
waking. I was going to be sick. We were clear of Asgard

then, past Vanaheim and Aflheim; the realms
of the gods. By Midgard. The endless ride,
the slide of my eyes between the bag and the abyss, the roll

as the body parts tried to break free. On my front, blood
cold-sticky. The head writhed, I imagined lips pulled back
from the teeth; I felt hate coming at me. Who could have believed

severed bits would reanimate when the body did?
I had been right not to drop the sodden sack down
into the Cloud river from the Rainbow bridge, don't

think I hadn't thought of the easy thing to do. I felt
a searing pain on my left breast and flailed;
almost falling off with the force

of what I realized was a bite. We were coming
close to Jotunheim; I had to get the head under control.
What could I tie the bag with? I had to concentrate

on my *seithr* of **down down**. No belt. No cloak. I had
no reins. The mare shuddered; she'd been bitten. I smashed a hard
elbow into the sack. I called to the mare, *Hold*

us level, Bright-mane. I took my boot knife and, with
regret, sawed off my mouse-brown braid. That was
my only beauty, the sheen and the length of it wound

now into a rope. I had meant only to tie the bag shut
so I could dangle it without being bitten, but another snap
from the murderer's head at my arm, and a soaring

fury gave me strength to gag the head, force
the bag-material deep down the throat as I could, then finish
winding and twining it with my braid. I was filled

with the urgency of revenge; it felt worse
than I could have imagined. Then I lowered the worsted
bag, tied with more knots than Odin has names, and whistled

to Bright-mane. *Now, let's try this again.* She pranced down as
if she were laughing. Past Jotunheim. By Nidavellir, a
Realm where my fathers, the dwarrow kings, lived among

those tall blue mountains I could see around the Tree's
curve of trunk. The braid-rope was working. The
sack swung in sickening arcs, but they

stayed away from flesh. And the woven bag couldn't be chewed
through with the head gagged. We'd got further than I could
have believed. We were opposite the Fire Realm when two crisp

black shapes scissored by us, *whock whock*, and away. Odin's ravens
going to report back. Then Muspelheim dwindled, its raving
orange glow giving way to black. Two more Realms

to go. I tried not to think of how much faster Sleipnir
was than any other skyhorse, including my sweet
mare. It was frosty now. The abyss breathed up sliced

mint and hard snow at us. I was a fool for my light
clothes. Opposite Helheim, the sky leveling
off to a dreary blue, all those souls lingering

in two-faced Hel's Realm. Queen of the dead,
one half alive, the other livid with decay. Down
the steep air to Niflheim, where ice dreamed

itself alive and utter darkness brooded. This
at least I was prepared for. I sang. The Norns had told
me that when the heart utterly fails, the thread

of hope brought by singing creates light. And it was so;
a tiny glow about Bright-mane's neck made my destiny sigh
and uncurl with relief. I wondered: would we freeze solid

before we reached the Nidhogg dragon, who gnawed the Tree's
roots? Brutal chill bit us. We could smell the dragon, black rot threading
rank through mint. Would it accept our gift or take us too?

Pale puffs of mist curled by Bright-mane. We could see
at least an arm's length around us now. It seemed
less icy. Were we getting close to the great spring

where twenty-six rivers pour out? Rivers couldn't be
frozen and flow. It seems foolish, but I clung to that blighted
idea; I was starving and so chilled I could barely

clutch the neck of my brave-hearted mare. My hands were
stiff as saplings. I was dispirited to my core by the wretched
smell and darkness like a thief. Maybe it was despair wafting

down spiderweb-sticky from Hel. If it was just myself, maybe
I would have given up, but under me, Bright-mane moved
ahead into the void and she was here because I'd asked more

of her than anyone ever had of a skyhorse, so for love
of her I shook myself, said aloud, *I will reach toward light
because I am sickened by the reverberation of this lethal*

*blood on blood that has been my life. Somewhere there
is a place of sun and meadows with the joyous tilt
of skyhorses playing in spruce-scented air. I want to find that*

*green place with you and Sleipnir and speak
a language that has no word for vengeance, a safe
place where we will act and speak*

with kindness. And it seemed to me then that the pouch
on my belt that held Ymir's piece
of skull, warmed as if invisible sun pierced

through nine-fingered leaves. Below us the head jerked
and I knew, eyes near watering, we couldn't rest yet. Jagged
ground appeared beneath us, a charcoal jumble

of boulders and an unlit hall the bulk of three whales. I strained
to see, yes, there was an oily gleam of water beside it. I shuddered.
This must be Náströnd, Dead Body Shore.

Prophecies said the hall doors faced north and the roof was
woven of serpents' backs like a wattle house. This was true. Weird
shrieks rose to us. Only grey, only flat in all this dim wasteland.

No trees, no mountains, no grass. Only Bright-mane and
I were alive in all this dire plain. I knew this with arctic
certainty. This was a cursed place. *We are*

going further, I told the skyhorse. *Can you smell*
water? We are looking for the largest spring
in all the Realms. Don't be startled

by hissing. Under Hvergelmir is the one we are
coming to see. We were stepping level then and,
as Bright-mane took my meaning, she shuddered in answer.

Whatever lithe currents of air skyhorses trod
gave up in the breathless twilight,
the dank tracery of rot, the treacherous

glue of despair at this lowest of Realms. We
stumbled across frost-rimed slag; I worried
Bright-mane would twist a leg on the wicked

slicks of mounded boulders,
some knee-high, others the size of an ice-bear.
When we saw the sheen of a tiny pool, Bright-

mane stopped. I slid off her back, tested
the standing water with one finger. It tasted
stale but we were so harshly thirsty

we gulped it down. It burned in my
stomach. The dim plain looked like motionless
animals had halted momentarily

and might come to life in a welter of squeals
and piping cries at any time. An hour later, we smelled
Hvergelmir. A wholesomeness, a sweetness

to the spring made my sore eyes water.
It made me remember the green wide
fields I had promised Bright-mane, the whiskery

silk of Sleipnir's nose. We heard a voice.
I couldn't make out what it was saying, but the very
intensity of its sadness slid up and down my nerves like a vane

screeching in the wind. Then it stopped. There was
only the click and slither of hooves, my weary
breaths and the mare's. We went

on for hours, it felt like. We could hear a roar
now, and the air felt wetter. These rivers
were the great ones of the Realms;

the ground shook with the drive of their flowing.
But the lament? Gone. Finally
we could see a brighter force

against what passed for sky. Almost silver,
it plumed up and we knew it for the spring
Hvergelmir. How strange such life-water sprang

from this desolation. Bright-mane took us
to the edge of the cataract; it went up
like a waterfall in reverse, a fountain with unlimited

power. We stopped, soaked, and I called
reluctantly, *Nidhogg*. Nothing. So I cried
again, louder, my voice tattered against the cold

and rumble of the spring. And a voice answered,
Over here. Who are you? It sounded like a
young girl. Shivering, we wheeled against

the fierceness of the spray toward the being I
had been brought up to despise, this dragon inside
the spring who gnawed the root of the World Tree, the inky

root of which was in fact plunging into Hvergelmir.
I'd taken it for a mountain, the wood was black and huge,
only now I could see the curve and twist, the hatching

of scales on the bark. And then two amber lights blazed
up and I realized what I'd taken for the root was the black
of the dragon Nidhogg, and those were its eyes before

us. The dragon flapped into the air, settled by the spring, said
in that high girly voice, *You're a gift for me!* All the prophecies swore
it wasn't until The Last Battle the dragon would be set free,[5] but she

hadn't read them. There Bright-mane and I were,
smelling like food. Nidhogg smacked her clawed paws, whistled
with joy. *Ratatoskr told me you were coming but I didn't know whether*

to believe that drill-tooth liar. Odin's girl,
are you? Nidhogg asked. *You'll taste so good.*
She sighed. *I'll remember you and this gorge-*

pleasing horse. That brought me out of my daze. *Malice Striker,*
we are not for you, I said, trying not to piss myself for sheer
terror. It heartened me slightly

the dragon had got my father wrong. *You are here for oath-*
breakers and murderers. That beaky immense face, oval
as a shield and three times the size of the red door of

Freyja's hall, blinked. *You are going to stop ME?*
Nidhogg's head looked like the most massive
and evil of turtles. She clacked her jaws; I glimpsed mighty

bony plates rather than fangs. The stench had me swaying
on Bright-mane's back. *I've brought you something*
you've never tasted before, I said.

I saw a pale roil inside the dragon's burrow once
my eyes adjusted. Snakes. It was an ocean of
them; thousands thrashed. As well as this infestation, one

hundred or more serpents thrust out their heads from holes in the slag.
The prophecies had this right, I remembered now: they said,
The number of snakes is countless. Their heavings are a loathsome sight.

The dragon blew out her breath. *Puhh.* My poor
Bright-mane quivered. *I can smell that paltry
bag. I can grind you all down without pausing*

to burp. I said with great politeness, *This is true,
most awe-inspiring of dragons.* Nidhogg clapped her two
front paws together again. *So what's to*

*stop me? Even Thor with his thunderbolts
couldn't—And you're a nothing. No one in bright
Asgard misses you.* This hissed with a venom that almost blew

me from Bright-mane's neck but still in that little
voice that came so oddly from the loathsome
white-slimed maw. I lifted both hands. The bag I held looked

wet with fresh blood. *You
are right, of course, Malice Striker. But if you
devour us now, won't you always wonder why I came to you?*

I dropped my voice. *You'll wake at night and say "I wish
I'd listened to that girl." For it's been a long while
since anyone told you a story, hasn't it? Who*

*else in all the time you've fed on corpses
has come to visit Hvergelmir?* The dragon ran a claw
across one cheek plate and was silent. *A century?*

I asked. *Never? An unfinished story is an itch*
that can never be scratched. It's an irritation
that can only be soothed by finding out what in

the world happens next and next after that.
In this bag is a head that belongs to a body which, thanks
to Odin, is still alive. Also the reðri and the bǫllr of the

murderer of my sister-friend. He was an oath-breaker
who fooled even the high gods. The amber eyes blazed;
Fooled even Odin, hey? I nodded. *I'll bargain*

with you, dragon. I'll give you the story, all
the delicious details, if you grant us safe away
from this place. Nidhogg scratched an

eyelid. *You're a killer. Why not just eat*
you? I hadn't expected to be so accused. The einherjar
the head belonged to was the finest of Freyja's elite,

I said. *Her commander. Do you think I could*
kill him? But wouldn't you like to know how I came
by his head? Nidhogg sighed. *You claim*

you didn't murder him? I nodded. Nidhogg thrust
out a forked tongue to lick the air. Under her, the
coil of luminous snakes writhed. *I taste the truth.*

I said to her, *And yet I have taken revenge*
for my friend. The dragon perked up. *Revenge?*
I nodded. *So how does this murderer remain*

alive? Nidhogg asked. *You're sure*
you'll tell me every detail? You'll speak
until I have no more questions? We both swore.

The dragon slid a shoulder up, scritched dripping claws
along one armoured forelimb. Anyone could
tell she had no intention of cleaving

to a promise. But I pretended to believe; got her to swear by
her hope of The Last Battle—carnage to her is as breathing
to us—and the great and horrible ship *Naglfar* which will bring

armies of the evil dead to fight in The Last Battle—and
the Fire-god Surt, that she would agree
to let Bright-mane and I go unharmed at

the close of my story. As we spoke, the dragon wove strange
and dizzying patterns with her snaky
neck against the dim sky until I felt half stupefied.

But I had wits enough to dismount and whisper
to Bright-mane before I wished her away, *Tell Sleipnir what*
has happened. You can wait until my wyrd

is done, but go so far from the dragon, I'm only
a dot to you. Then I told vast Nidhogg the story of
Krista's death and what I'd done. She opened

her mouth and gnashed her grinding plates
with glee, laughed like the clash of rusty chains. *You please*
me, she said at last. *You brought me property*

that belongs to Odin himself. Alive and dead, mm. She seemed to
have a fixed hatred of the All-Father. Her tail thrashed
and as the snakes cleared in her dark hole, I saw a tall

stack of corpses; the dead-reek was so vile,
each in-drawn breath felt like tasting foul vinegar.
I pulled out Anfinn's head, held it up, let the vast

horror of where we were seize him. *We're*
in Hvergelmir, I said. *Despair.* This was the end, utter winter-
night desolation for the damned that we

—all Asgard—feared. *Meet Nidhogg.* I tossed the head
into the dragon's mouth, dark red and holding
open. Then I threw the bag. Nidhogg moved her jaws, made hissy

sounds of pleasure, swallowed. Shaking, I watched the
slobber-smeared jaws stop, the amber eyes turn
to me. She'd known when I sent Bright-mane to

safety that I knew my death was an avalanche in slow
ice-shattering motion, cascading upon me. Why should
a dragon who sucked on corpses be stopped

by a vow? Pallid snake-heads popped up and down
from burrows. The dull sky never changed. I was drenched
with spray. I would not run from my destiny, nor disgrace

myself. I stood and faced the dragon, who keened, the
sound that far off, had so disturbed Bright-mane and me. This
time, beside her, the sorrow was enough to tear

out the heart from a person and filet it. *I gave you an
oath*, black Nidhogg said. *I am the weight that crushes all
breakers of promises. A promise is the ridge beam that holds up a*

*whole roof. I believe in ridge beams above all. Cunning girl. You said "safe
away from this place" so now I must gift you with wind for the skyhorse.
See if Odin is as merciful as the one you name "Malice Striker."*

Nidhogg leapt into the air then, fanned her wings and blew me,
stumbling, to Bright-mane. She hissed, *You're hideous, the meat
of you is all the wrong colours. Everyone in Asgard calls you a monster.*

ᛋ

I couldn't go further than Nidavellir, where I collapsed.
My fathers identified me by the gold cuff they'd crafted.
Their kindness to me, the lost daughter that clearly

fate had brought to them, was like being in a room with
a crackling fire on a winter day. They told me Freyja withstood
many pleas for me to live with them. But their wives,

childless, hated me as deeply as when crusts of rock
part from one another and the bitter tang of magma running
molten chokes the breath. So really,

I understood my mother saying no. I wondered how long
the wives would let me live if I tried to stay in Nidavellir, its lambent
bowl of stone peaks open to the sun, sweet with the lilt

of the mountains' clean stone breath. Even thinking about
going back to Asgard filled me with grey dread. But, after
a week, Odin's ravens dive-bombed me. I understood a

summons when I saw one. Too quickly, Bright-mane and I found
ourselves at the Rainbow bridge at the curve where it fastens
on the birch forest side. Heimdall waited mid-bridge, fidgeting

with a spear. Had Odin barred me from returning?
Swoops of light from the blade reflected
on Bright-mane's neck, the floating prisms of restless

colour that gave the bridge its name, hurled up in spray
from the Cloud river. *Your sword, Sigrene*, Heimdall said.
I unsheathed my boot knife, held it to him hilt first. *So*

it's bad? I asked, looking at his face, its weary
blaze like the heart of a forge. He whistled
then, and in the air, I saw a whirl

of skyhorses and Valkyries. They galloped down,
hooves striking the bridge deck in drum-cracks, faced us in double
rows. In front, the dun of Freyja's captain danced,

blonde Berglín who'd said she'd kill me.
I thought of my fathers' Realm then, blue mountains
as alive as our trees, wished myself

back there. It hurt that Heimdall had given
me no warning; I'd thought of him as the one god
who was my friend. Odin I knew I couldn't get

away from in any Realm, but being cut down by
my teachers—*Sigrene*, Berglín called. *The bag*
you carried with you when you left, what became

of it? Bright-mane pranced. I glanced
back, saw Heimdall barred our way behind. *I gave
it to Nidhogg, I said. The dragon gulped it down and gifted*

us with wind under Bright-mane's hooves. The line
of skyhorses and Valkyries clattered closer. *That one[6] is no longer
living?* Berglín asked, meaning Anfinn. I was caught like

bait in the jaws of a trap. I raised my voice, said,
*What I took of that murderer is now shit
where the snakes of Hvergelmir nest on top.* The Valkyries screamed

loud enough to terrify a colony of seabirds—but
my teachers were saying *Yes! Good!* Their blades
whipped out to catch the sun. I couldn't believe

it, they saluted me! Heimdall whacked
my shoulder so hard I came near to winding
up face-down on the bridge, hearing *Sigrene, I was so worried.*

I woke with a start that night, summoned
by a taut line that tugged at my forehead, sure
it was Odin. The pull had his star-energy, the swift

sizzle-lightning feel of the All-Father. Half-drunk, I reeled
outside Sessrúmnir's riveted door. Six shadows rose
black behind me; there was no moon but I could feel the raw

energy of the men, just see the darker blots of bodies against
the chill night. Terror twisted in my guts like an adder,
then a voice said, *We're here for what you did for Krista*, and

I realized it was Thorvald. *We applaud your vengeance. We'll
protect you.* The men followed as I led the way to Valhalla without
a word more spoken. It was a half hour's walk over rough wavering

ground, though that was likely the mead I'd drunk.
Or my shame at having pissed on Thorvald the day
the other uncles had hacked him apart, him denying

he'd ever hurt Krista. His lover. I no longer cared. At
Valhalla's door, Thorvald said, *We'll wait.* I almost
said, *Why?* but clamped my lips shut around

that hard question and nodded. You'd think I'd outgrow
fear, but it didn't seem to happen. Odin
waited inside his high hall. Firelight outlined

him, lounging in his chair made to look like a tree
trunk, though it was worked gold. The tight
line between us hummed with tension.

I let it pull me to him and stopped a sword's bright length
away. Not that a weapon mattered to the Lord
of Asgard. It was dim. Odin glowered at me, looked

at the fire, which leaped and began to burn like
a barn when raiders torch it. I lowered
my eyes, knowing the reckoning had arrived. Odin said at last,

*You took my champion's head. The Valkyries have
forgotten they hated you. All Asgard heaves
with your new-woven name, the one you came home*

with from Urd's Well. Sigrene. He said this with
such ice I lifted my eyes. A mistake. His one eye whirled
constellations and I thwacked hard onto a mead-bench, wishing

I had better sense or that he would kill me quickly. *You
refused the wergild I asked for,* I protested. Odin said, *You've
acted with a courage to be proud of. But rashly.* Yellow

firelight pushed bright warmth
against my legs. I let silence widen
like a long meadow between us: wanting

this to be over. *The head of my champion
is wergild I refused,* the All-Father said. *Can
you claim that I was not clear?*

I swallowed, said, *You were clear.* The pouch holding Opna
warmed. Odin's eyes went to it. *What's that?* I offered
him the dust-coloured pouch. He opened

the layers with care, held up the shard of skull to
the firelight. *I recognize this,*
he said, as well he might, his had been the

hand to strike Ymir's neck from his shoulders. *Tell me the whole story
of your journey,* Odin said. *Every detail. It might seem
like nothing, but at Ragnarök, the smallest*

knife of knowledge may tilt the battle in our favour.
Morning seeped grey around the edges of the five
doors of Valhalla by the time I had finished. They were fine

yew wood from Nidavellir, rubbed with oil and with bronze
dwarrow-made hinges, ornate, long as my arm. Odin had bent
such attention on my words, in the dawn light I felt bruised

from the force of his focus. *And so*, he said, targeting
strategy as always. *Nidhogg wings free.* I thought,
Odin will never be on my side. The All-Father said, *This*

*was not foretold by Mimir until the end of days. We must be close to
to that time when all Asgard will fight together.* I sighed. *I told
you of my vision in Nifelheim, of green fields and sun, the tether*

of a gold not made with hands. It's a summons. I accepted
that coin, mighty Odin. I am not able to spend any
other. I have avenged by sister-friend's death. As best as I'm able

I will keep my promise to Bright-mane and Sleipnir of the seithr-
charged vision that showed itself to me. *I have satisfied*
honour. The Norns have shown me how even the smallest

of changes affect the colours and patterns of the stories we live.
I must bend my life-flame to serve peace. Odin grunted. He wasn't
angry that I could see, just kept rolling Ymir's bone one way

and then the other in his palms. *Did the Vanir tell*
you what this is for? I shook my head. *He told*
me he didn't know. Odin asked, *Are you offering it to*

to me? I sighed. *I was hoping for more*
of a bargain, I said. Odin snorted. *You mean,*
for your life? I looked up to the roof beam. Hadn't Malice

Striker said, "See if Odin is as merciful as me?" *No,*
for Sleipnir's. The All-Father rolled the bit of skull in its neat
twist of cloth, packed it away, handed it to me. *I don't need*

this. Now I heard the patter of ash leaves at the Urd's Well,
urgency gripped me the way an owl clamps onto a mouse. What
was I supposed to remember? *Is there a favour I might do for you, wisest*

of gods? I asked. *About Tyr, perhaps?* Odin's look
of sorrow was so strong, I could've leaned
against it like an ice-wind at dark midwinter.

What I meant, I had only the haziest of memories. But
my destiny leapt as I spoke; this was the beginning
of a new thread on the World Loom. I drew a breath,

invoked *seithr* and **pulled** with all the force I could manage on
the blessing the Norns had sent me away with. *Ah*, Odin
said. *A favour. I see the weaving now. The pouch on*

your belt is a sign. It's sky and skull and Tree,
a gift from this World to the next. Its purpose is to
open. Bury it if you manage to get through.

I smelled grease and blood sausage, heard the clatter of
pans in the kitchen. I followed ash-haired Odin
in his blue cloak and we paced outside

into the morning mist. I was not surprised
when the All-Father took us to where Sleipnir
cropped grass with Bright-mane and three smaller

mares. He said, *The favour is about the Wolf.* The skyhorses moved
to stand in a circle about us. Like haunts, mist
scudded along the field, tumbling mysterious

spheres close to the ground, without
any wind moving it I could feel, damp and white
when the swirls sifted by my legs. I echoed, *The Wolf?*

You are going to leave Asgard forever, Odin said.
I had barely reached womanhood; I shrank
from the loss of everything I knew but I squeezed

out, *Is it written?* Odin huffed out a breath,
said, *By me it is.* In the air, he sketched out the bold
amber of runes. They carried the deep hum of bees

and the scent of honey. The runes hung twisting while
the All-Father looked at me. Yes, I whispered.
This weaving was what I had seen, wasn't

it? He said, *I need Sleipnir for Ragnarök. When I fall
to the Wolf, and the wind knows my name no more, then find
Sleipnir and take him from that hard-fought and fiercest*

of battles. None of the skyhorses flicked an ear. I studied
Odin's lustrous boots. He cleared his throat; I slitted
my eyes. *I will also give you the mare you call Bright-mane.* I said

nothing. *All right*, the All-Father grumbled. *And
the other mares in foal.* Now the skyhorses shifted. I asked,
How many? He said, *Six.* Dread answered

me; I felt sick. This was too generous. I felt the way
a seal might at a breathing hole, knowing danger was
looming: the black nose of an ice-bear waiting.

Odin's favour would be huge. This bad
unknown asking hung in the air, invisible as the barely
there wind that bowled the mist-balls. I bent

my head. Ragnarök must be close indeed to unlock Odin's desire
to own his horse even beyond death, the All-Father's doom
becoming Sleipnir's. Only, I told myself, I would dart down

to save my skyhorse. I tested further: *What about the colts too
young to be ridden?* wondering if I'd gone too far this time.
You can have them, Odin said, confirming for me the

nearness of the end. And then he fixed me
with his one terrible eye. *This favour will help many,*
he said. *I have been generous.* I thought, *maybe,*

then looked into the skyhorses' long-fringed eyes.
The air between us hummed sweet with trust. Even
without knowing what Odin wanted, I agreed. Every

nerve was shrieking, but I'd glimpsed the World
Loom and said yes there. So the hard destiny woven
between me and the Wolf pulled taut in the Loom's web.

PART 3

ODIN'S FAVOUR

᛫

Loki's eyes glittered above me, upside down, like sun
glancing on lapis lazuli, hectic blue. *Stay still*, he commanded. I sat
unmoving on the coping around Urd's Well. Unseen *seithr*

frothed in air thick enough to spoon. Then Odin's
face swam into view. I dropped my eyes, unwilling to open
myself to that hard dizziness his star-gaze often

provoked; it would not be smart to find out what
would happen if I toppled backward. The Well
might tease me into such tiny shards of light no one would

know I had ever lived. I understood the two wanted to
change my body to look like Tyr's, most honourable of the
Aesir. What did they want from me then?

Tyr was the high gods' warlord: I wouldn't do well
if I got called on to fight. Out of all the Aesir, he wouldn't
cheat; he was as reliably kind as a hot spring is to weary

travellers. I had agreed to Odin's favour—his words—
to save Sleipnir and Bright-mane, wisest
and dearest of skyhorses. With death the alternative, who

wouldn't chance a favour? A person had to
make that moment count when we flared out like an ember tossed
into dark ocean. So I held still as Odin touched

my face with hands like live coals. I thought of Sleipnir and
breathed out along the line of light that arced between us, and
breathed out again, clenched the Well's coping as

if   cold   black   stone
could   strengthen
me   and   the   shriek

of pain that almost escaped sank rasping to the back
of my throat and Odin said, *That's better,*
released me. Ah. I could breathe

like a summer morning. The whole
of creation grew luminous. Every leaf on the World
Tree hummed with life. Grass whirled with

a transparent dance and yet didn't move. It was as
though everything I saw was saturated with meaning and
each colour was so fresh it was only at

that moment springing into being. I saw as gods did
and it was dazzling. *It worked,* Loki said, eyes darting
sideways. His scarred mouth stretched into a downward

smile. Energy zipped yellow about his face like terrible
wasps, angry, alert. I wondered if it was true that
Tyr was Odin's son, what agonizing thing

I was supposed to do. Two days later,
I found out. We rode down the Tree, almost lovelier
to my Tyr-sight than I could bear. I leaned

forward in my high skysaddle stunned with the fullness
and patterned spin of life, the stars in Ginnungagap, the fresh
scent of mint from the cold Void. I felt

I knew now why Odin wanted so desperately to keep
the Realms safe, why his whole being was keyed
to protect. The final slam of Ragnarök would kill

life in all the Realms. Our ride took us far north in Midgard
where icebergs floated, lonely cliffs on a grey sea. Misgivings
made me sour. We were going to see Finn, that much

the gods had told me. Loki had left us.
Thor met us on Lyngvi Island, ugly
with its lack of trees, though I sensed the sea that undid

its white wave belt on the islands and the bergs about us was
thrashing with fish and seals with razored teeth. While
Thor bellowed greetings, I saw the Wolf coming, winding

through snow and beach-weed, a thunderbolt
in slow motion, so glorious he made my throat tighten
with longing to touch him. Finn towered

over Sleipnir, who stepped sideways under Odin, laid
his ears back. As Odin rode the stallion, so I led
my strange large Tyr-body, though the god-senses loaned

to me so confused me I felt like a falling star
in vast night. The Wolf leapt and stood, paws on my shoulders,
laughing above my face. I had been coached, I shouted

Finn! reached up to thump his shoulders. His coat was as glossy
and soft as I remembered though I grumbled,
Pwah, whale-breath, and he grinned

and his tail beat so strongly I could hear air
sighing: hadn't Tyr been the only god in Asgard
who'd dared bring him food, water, and

insist the Wolf be treated kindly? I had no idea
what Odin was up to, but I liked Finn and, idiot
that I was, I thought *I will behave with honour, I*

can make this turn out all right. And of course this
was what the gods counted on. My destiny tore
by, lamenting; I saw it and stood taller.

Hours of persuasion passed; the gods were trying to chain
Finn. With him bound, the years until Ragnarök would creep
toward us, rather than leap, or so subtle Odin was convinced.

The prophecies were clear: Ragnarok wouldn't start until Finn
ran wild. The Wolf would eat the sun and moon because finally
he would be so immense, his back would touch the flaming

sky. Together Finn and I sat on the desolate
stone with wind-hammered waves *hisshing* in. Dog-like,
the Wolf leaned on me, head taller than mine, devotion

so blatant I thought he mocked us all.
But he was warm. His fur smelled of frost-flowers and air
so I let him stay leaning. Finn said, *I was able*

to break Loeðing. Then I broke Drómi. These were chains
the gods had brought to him before, I realized as the cold
afternoon darkened. Thor taunted him, saying, *Those, children*

could break. Finn snarled, *But not you, for you showed me*
those iron fetters were beyond your mettle.
Odin said, *Your renown has gone far. But you realize you've met*

your match. That's all right. Nothing to be ashamed of.
While his words were meant for Finn, I felt an opening
in my heart tremble in shame: it was outrageous

the gods kept goading him. *Why don't we just*
go home? I asked. I shrugged off the Wolf's weight, jumped
to my feet. *This has gone on long enough. Finn's quite justified*

in saying no, he doesn't want to put on Gleipnir. It looks
like a ribbon anyway. He's too dignified for a little
ribbon. Thor said, *You're right. It's too girly. It'd look*

sweet, though. Then snickered in a way that could take the bristles
off a wild boar. *Finn's afraid of looking like a bee-yee-you-ti-ful*
girl wolf. Coward. Finn wrinkled his lips back

from his teeth; Thor's hand dropped to his hammer.
I thought, the only reason Finn's put up with this horrible
teasing for so long is he's lonely. Odin's hands

trickled Gleipnir from palm to palm. It was silky;
I had touched the chain earlier. Had my fathers made it? Silly
to feel a stir of pride when I thought of the surpassing

skill dwarrows have in fashioning metal. *It's a trick*, Finn
said. *You're out to get me. Why should I feel*
trust for any of you? His yellow eyes locked fierce

on me. I sighed. He was right. We were
all on our feet then. The ice-breath of the bergs was wicked.
Let's just go home, I said again. Finn howled and whirled

nose to tail, nose to tail, spinning like a puppy, *But
for me there is no home!* And his desolation near broke
my heart. *No chain on me*, he snarled, *unless someone's brave*

enough to put their right hand in my mouth. Thor shook
his head. *You'd bite my hammer hand for spite
if you didn't pop that ribbon off first thing*, he said.

Odin said, *Let me think.* And we stood there with night
coming on like a death. Sleipnir's ears flicked and I knew
then what was being asked of me. The full price necessary

for honour, for Sleipnir and Bright-mane who had carried me.
But I waited until my destiny moved
sure inside me. I said, *I will put my sword hand in your mouth,*

and walked to Finn who accepted it. Odin took
the chain Gleipnir and wound it around the legs of the
Wolf. It shut soft as a moth's wing touching

the lit edges of a door. *Is Gleipnir made of gold?*
I asked. Finn shuddered, said thickly around my grabbed
hand, *Don't like it.* He pulled hard. The chain grew

shorter. Finn was hobbled. He howled and tried
again. My hand was bruised from the force of his teeth
but he did not draw blood. The chain drew tighter

on him; he was bent like a bow now and my heart
tensed with pity. Thor said, *You are strong, Wolf.* His hand
stroked his hammer. *But would you know the whole*

of what Gleipnir is made from? Finn said, *I would.*
And he made an effort so mighty drool foamed in wide
sprays around us on the beach, but the fetter wouldn't

break, only tightened. The Wolf looked at me
with such desolation in his eyes that I must
blink water from my own. *What is Gleipnir made*

from? Finn mumbled. And though his body
trembled with how tight the fetters were bonding
him, still he did not draw blood.

Thor said, *Gleipnir is made from:*
the sound of a cat's footfall,
the beard of a woman,
the roots of a mountain,
the sinews of a bear,
the breath of a fish,
the spittle of a bird.

Finn groaned. *I will try harder then. Move*
with me, Tyr. And I let him dance me,
as, my sword hand in his mouth,

he bent, grunted, strained and this time
his teeth met through bone. This time
I was dragged like a rag through

arc after arc of him trying to free himself and finally
Finn stood, sides heaving, unable to force
Gleipnir apart. Then Wolf bit off my hand. The fierce

shock of that loss sent me backward, blood
geysering from my wrist-stump on the dark beach.
I'd acted just like Tyr would have. I couldn't be bitter.

My fathers. How I love them. Odin
said he'd aimed us for their kingdom; I worried it was only
as ruse but when I see my fathers' faces, frowning, worried, oh

relief reels me in grey circles, near chokes me.

Bitter willow for pain and

. . .

. . . my own arm. Not Tyr's long one. But missing my *seithr* hand
my sword hand my hand for eating for wi. . .

. . . warm at last

I am a price. I was beguiled. I will never be famous
for losing my hand to a Wolf who trusted me and was fooled.
A stick jammed upright in sand, I howl as the agony wind flays

      bark

            Pain   eats you.   Even breathing
         But   herbs   torment   slow   a battering
            can endure.   bargain.

            remind   self   each breath

                ᛋ

Thor had staunched the bright spurting, kept me
upright in the long ride, but my wrist was a mess.
Pain defined each breath. Every medicine

my fathers tried, failed. I heard them whisper, *Poison.*
Finn was brother to the Jormundgand serpent, poison
was in their natures, never mind their teeth. My passage

toward death led me down dim hallways with only closed
doors; I spun in dreams as painful as a cloak
of thistles worn next to the skin. My eyes closed.

My stump grew swollen and hot. Red streaks shot
up my arm. My fathers thought I would die by sunset.
Then Freyja whirled in with her Gib-cats, stalked

into my room in Nidavellir, that scoured bowl in the mountains
called Sun's Roof, where my fathers reigned. I mumbled
when I saw Freyja, thinking I was dreaming. My mother

was wreathed in *seithr* so bright it hurt me when
she flung open the door, hair tips wriggling
like snakes; that's how furious she was

with me, not with Odin, which I thought unfair but
didn't have enough voice to tell her. Had Freyja forgiven my birth?
At least my mother had come, and now she bent

over me, smelling like moonflowers. When she saw my
breaths shallow as bubbles and my wrist stump purple,
she said, quiet as a hunting cat, *What happened? Powerful*

Odin said only she'd lost a hand. My fathers told her.
Freyja asked my fathers to make a copper hook
for me. They forged it with *seithr*, pure as sunrise, heated

with Freyja's spells until it gleamed so bright I couldn't
look at it. When she pressed the hook into my wrist, I cried
out high and thin as a rabbit's death-scream. I called

for my fathers, and, murmuring, the four held
me still. *This will make it better*, Dvalinn said, his
voice humming with my torment. And the hurting

stopped. I panted, sucking in air like
a child when it tries to calm. My mother said, *Look
how the swelling has gone down.* We all looked

at my stump, the copper curving from healed skin
as though it had grown there and so
beautiful, no pain, no pain at all. Seldom

has a pleasure been so acute for me as that
stopping of pain. The sun poured hot honey through
the bound air of the light shafts. I turned

my wrist; it didn't hurt. *It feels like my hand is still
attached*, I said. Freyja said, *But you'll have to spin
seithr left-handed from now on.* Berling laughed: *That scowl*

on your face says you're going to live. And he hugged
me more gently than he'd ever done. Alfrik held
my shoulders, asked, *Is it true the Wolf actually ate your hand?*

I grimaced. *Fair—*, I started to say,
but my words fused: my jaws snapped
shut. When I tried to nod, my neck seized.

Freyja screwed one eye shut to mimic the All-
Father. I blinked. That was all I could do. Alfrik's
eyes reddened. From then on, there were holes in memory we all

fell into. Moths ate our words. Only images remained.
Light flashed from my copper hook as I twisted it in rich
sun. I couldn't say *Wolf* or *slow to draw blood* but I remembered.

We six were the only ones who'd ever remember.

So many sadnesses to warm
yourself at. Like a leaping fire

they spit sparks and you can believe
such lit griefs beautiful,

the way the handle of a favourite blade
is beautiful, nestled into the hand,

its smooth haft promising red joy.
Even now, when I have foresworn

killing, I hunger for that narrow
certainty where the world funnels

down to only the precision of movement,
breath, the ice-flick of terror.

Either I won that fight,
or it would be my head

jammed onto a stake outside the hall
for ravens and ants to ravage.

Did you know that when you cut off
a head and call the name it answered to

among the living,
the head opens its eyes and looks at you?

After a moment, the head slumps
into stillness. It won't rouse again.

Imagine how long that moment

stretches   out.

My teachers with blades
were glacier-hearted Valkyries.

They taught me steel
was the most final of answers

to men who thought women
ripe apples on a tree.

I would be sorry to tell
of the games that shield-maids played

with men's heads.

I told none of this to the holy man I met
after Ragnarök when the skyhorses and I passed
through into the new green world.

Brendan stood barely taller than me
but the peace of the earth flowed
through him; I could see lines of force.

He looked at my silver skin,
Addy's face like a grim, Sleipnir's oozing wounds,
the blood on my hands and hook from tending him,

and said, *Be welcome.* His brown-robed fellows
had run, screaming. I asked for water and grazing
for the skyhorses, who stood, heads hanging.

He nodded. *Surely it's a great*
story you have to tell, he said. *You've been hard*
pressed this winter. And perhaps a wash for yourself?

The kindness in his tone made my eyes sting.
I wouldn't speak about the Last Battle to Brendan.
Nor will I now, that wailing

world's end, huge and fiery as a comet
striking the chest.
I still see brave Grímur fall, Buri protecting

him to the last, needle-clawed.
They were dead when I fought
my way to them. In my arms

Buri weighed less than a shawl.
As Odin had instructed me, when we reached the new
green country I buried the treasure

my Vanir kinsman had given me:
"A gift from this World to the next."
But I kept the woven blue wisp of blessing

Freyja had wrapped the box in. That was mine.
The runes read, *Clouds hide me, wind guide me,*
sky protect me from the breath of my enemies.

I never told Brendan my "great story."
I ate bread and honeycomb, eggs and plain soups
with the brothers and sisters—

that's what they said to call them—
who, circled, silent, eying me the way
dogs do before a fight, hackles raised, despite

Brendan's welcome. Sleipnir's slashes healed
slower than I liked. I cared for the skyhorses
and the other animals; everyone worked.

I was slow with a pitchfork. All I knew
was the way of the sword.
The skyhorses made the group decide

we were god-touched. Which, of course,
was true. On the morning Bright-mane and I circled
in the sky, a group of sisters

sat with me at lunch and asked questions
like what had happened to the skyhorses' wings?
Daily, I snuck Sleipnir half my oatmeal

until one morning Brendan caught me.
He put a hand on my arm. I could smell
the clean male scent of him. He smiled and said,

I'll show you the bag of oats in the stable.
I fumbled a gold ring off my arm, held
it out. Brendan shook his head until the brown beard

that foamed to his waist flapped. *No, you're "the Name*
in the mouth of friend and stranger."[7] *It's you*
who's gifting us by being here. And he saw me,

the way the gods had sometimes,
my short legs, my copper hook, the blue
and green sheen of my skin, but

he delighted in me the way a willow does in rain.
Later, I watched him pick up worms from the paths, put
them on the grass where they wouldn't get

stepped on. He smiled at worms
the way he smiled at me or the sun
coaxing steam from a damp hillside.

I fell in love with his laugh or maybe his eyes;
they were grey or blue on different days.
I didn't tell Brendan of the high gods' death.

When he talked to me of one god,
I managed not to laugh, asked,
Tell me about the peace I feel in you—

Was this the peace I'd felt in that sun-vision
I'd seen in the darkest level of rot-sour Niflheim?
By then, I knew I meant no more than a spray

of pink-flushed apple bloom to him,
but it's hard to retrieve a heart
once it's been given.

Out of curiosity, I spied on Brendan
for half a holy day: how did he behave
when no one was looking? I saw him nod

to a lamb and talk to an empty spring;
water flowed from it, but no
small mystery lived in it.

The country around Clonfert seethed with them
but he appeared not to see the mysteries' winks and waves.
He lost his temper with a brother

who'd been chivvying a young boy
until the boy's shoulders rounded; he was near tears.
I watched Brendan emerge from the kitchen

with half a loaf of bread, which he inhaled
in bites that left crumbs on his beard like snowflakes.
Was the bread taken or given?

I already knew Brendan ate
more than any two monks put together.
Energy sheeted from him; I thought

of Odin who'd smelled like lightning,
but then Brendan farted loudly,
smiled at the noise he made, adjusted his robe.

I coveted the shining peace he walked in.
It reached deeper than the roots of mountains.
Long ago, I had told Odin I'd accepted

the higher gold of peace
but I hadn't known where to find it.
Brendan, I thought, might show me.

Over the weeks I watched him, I noticed
when he laughed, it was with surprise, not malice.
I came to see that Brendan wore the sky as his cloak.

I thought the sky made a cold covering,
though its freshness was exhilarating.
At last I allowed him to trickle

water on my head and bless me
with the rune of four directions. The *seithr*
Brendan used was strange (and a man wielding it,

that prickled my neck) but I felt no harm.
He instructed me not to kill, told me the seven names
of god, and the colours of creation.

As a rowan wand bends to water,
Brendan was set on voyaging.
The navigator, his brothers called him.

He was looking for paradise;
he and the brothers had two currachs
ready to go. After the dragon ships

I was used to, currachs looked like slivers
waiting to flip, slim wicker baskets with tanned hides
for a hull. I kept my shudders to myself.

The gales of winter gave way
to spring. As well-fed skyhorses are likely
to do when the year warms and sap runs,

mine stepped up to the sky
and went galloping. The word angel began to be murmured
when overhead, the skyhorses left swooping shadows

on the green grass.
I mean, what else could they be?
It was time to let the wind take us away.

Brendan asked, *Sigrene, tell me as a kindness,*
which way does paradise lie?
I knew he would leave;

I could see the power in him shine and strain
toward the sunset. So I pointed there.
He laughed for joy. Hadn't a holy hermit told him

the same thing just the month before?
A week later, he and fourteen others
left for Galway to take the whale road.

Circling on Bright-mane, I watched from overhead.
Their currachs shrank until only the restless
grey of the billows was left.

Because of Brendan, I gave up using steel
as my talisman. He showed me the pattern
behind the sky, beautiful as light on water.

While I'll never go so far as to wear
the sky, like him, I do answer to the breathing light,
gold at the centre of all things.

I wonder though, that gold does not heal
my sorrows. Instead, I carry
them with me in a pocket, tiny as peas,

but smoldering like coals—
their burn goes through a palm
and out the other side.

What does a moment feel like
to a severed head?
          I think of this often.

ᛋ

A river runs through Asgard.
It's the Heilbrunr, green and
clean, fast-flowing. As a child, I played along

its banks and swam. Though when I see
one memory now—dappled Sleipnir
splashing with me neck deep in water—it seems

small as a gold coin held at arm's length. Where
is Krista, braid shiny as a chestnut? Why
isn't she with us in the chill thrill of water?

Is she working in the kitchen, while I, the goddess's
daughter, get to laze? In Heilbrunr's depths, green
and silver tiny fish flash light like knives. They grow

bold, come and tickle our legs, then dart
away in a fishcloud. The day is delicious
with air on bare skin, the collision of sun with dark

summer-sleeked ovals of water as I shade
my eyes on the shore, duck away as Sleipnir
rolls on hot sand. His dust puffs sideways. ·

On the warm beach I touch Sleipnir's
muzzle with tickly bumps of whiskers, seal-soft.
He lifts his head, whacks my face by accident so

hard I scold him; he rolls one black eye at me, wary.
The air is full of gold, the smell of wet horse. I float on what
I knew, memories sharp-edged as a whirl

of shore-birds ascending in a piping flock. All
levels swing from the great hinge of here-and-now, all
my younger selves are alert, anticipating

the futures to come. And, of course, failing.

GLOSSARY

Aesir (AA-seer): the high gods of Norse mythology.

Addý (ADD-dee): the murdered girl's mother and the protagonist's indentured servant.

Anfinn (ANNF-fin): commander of Freyja's army.

Asgard (ASS-gard): realm of the high gods, the Aesir.

Bifrost bridge (BI-frost): this span separated Asgard, the realm of the gods, from the other Realms.

bǫllr (BOWLrr): Old Norse slang for testicles.

Brísingamen (BRIZZ-in-gammon): a magical necklace of amber and gold fashioned by four dwarrow kings and acquired by Freyja, goddess of love, in return for sexual favours.

currach (KUHR-uh-kh): traditional Irish boat with a wooden frame, wrapped in leather.

einherjar (Ayn-HEER-ee-ar): especially valiant human warriors plucked after death from the battlefields by the Valkyries and resurrected to fight on the side of the gods at Ragnarök.

destiny: The Norse word was *wyrd*, fate. The original carries a freight of possibility the English lacks. *Wyrd* was, in a way, like a template, a shape for a person's life. The best way of dealing with it was to measure up. For example, it was Odin's fate to be killed by the Wolf. It was foretold. So when that end came, he would meet it with great bravery and dignity. But since Ragnarök, the Last Battle, was an event none of the gods wanted, Odin would do his best to make sure that end was delayed as long as possible.

dwarrow (DWWA-row): mountain-dwellers who specialized in the making of mighty weapons and jewelry. Another word for them is dwarves.

Fenrir Wolf (FEN-rear): wolf son of the god Loki and the giantess Angrboda. Prophecies foretold that the Wolf would bring about the destruction of all Realms, including Asgard, realm of the high gods. Those who knew the Wolf when he was a pup called him Finn.

Folkvangr (FOLK-vangrr): Odin's killing field.

Freyja (FRRAY-ya): Norse goddess of love and fertility. She was a shape-shifter, with a cloak of falcon feathers. Freyja also travelled in a chariot pulled by Gib-cats.

Frigg (Frigg): the highest ranking of the Norse goddesses. She was a prophet and wife to Odin, the chief god in the pantheon.

Gib-cats: These stripey animals, the size of cougars, drew Frejya's chariot between the Realms.

Ginnungagap (GIH-noong-ga-gap): the yawning Void.

Heimdall (HAYM-doll-er): the guardian god of Bifrost bridge, the only entry to Asgard, realm of the high gods.

Hvergelmir (WHEL-geh-meer): a spring where twenty-siz great rivers originated in the lowest underworld in Norse mythology.

The prophecies spoke of it fearfully. There was no worse place in the created universe.

Jera ⚡ (YARE-a): the run for harvest, cycle, rewards for past efforts, reap what you have sown.

Jotun (JO-tin): giants.

Jotunheim (JO-tin-hi-mm): realm of the giants.

Loki (LOW-kee): the trickster god in Norse mythology. Even though Odin had chained Loki after an especially vicious trick, and had a snake dripping venom on him, the All-Father still made use of Loki when he had need of him and unchained him from his cave. Loki was so relieved to escape the ongoing torture, he didn't ask many questions.

Loki was a shape-shifter. He was Fenrir Wolf's father and Sleipnir's mother.

Midgard (MID-gard): the human realm.

Mimir (ME-meer): the wisest of the Norse gods.

Mjolnir (My-YAWL-neer): Thor's magic hammer was a fearsome weapon, capable of leveling mountains.

Naglfar (NAG-far): a ghastly ship made entirely from the fingernails and toenails of the dead. It ferried the forces of evil to do battle with the gods at Ragnarök.

Nidavellir (NID-uh-vell-eer): realm of the dwarrows.

Nidhogg (NEETH-hog-ger): a fearsome dragon who lived in the lowest realm of the underworld. The prophecies said it sucked on corpses. Nidhogg was the special bane of oath-breakers and murderers.

Nine Realms[8]: These were held up by branches of the World Tree and divided into three main groupings: the realm of the gods, the human world, the underworld.

Realm of the gods

1.) Asgard, where the Aesir lived.
2.) Vanaheim, where the Vanir lived, elder gods who kept to themselves.
3.) Alfheim, home of the light elves, the *lios alfar*. I prefer to think of them as people in Iceland do, the Hiddenfolk.

The human world

4.) Midgard, the home of humans.
5.) Jotunheim, the home of ordinary giants (Jotuns).
6.) Nidavellir, where the dwarrows lived. Some commentators placed the dwarrows in Muspelheim, the fire-realm. I've chosen to believe they lived in Nidavellir.

The underworld

7.) Svartalfheim, where the dark elves, the *svart alfar*, lived. These are also Hiddenfolk. The fire giants and demons lived in Muspelheim.

8.) Helheim, where many but not all of the
dead went.

9.) Niflheim, the ice realm, was lowest of all levels. It
was the utter end of all things.

Norns (NOR-nn): the Norns are the Fates, Past, Present,
and Future. They lived at Urd's Well; Urd is the Past. Urd's
Well was sacred to the Aesir. Odin consulted the Norns there
several times a week. His strategy was two-fold: to stave off
end of the world, and, when that failed, to make the outcome
of battle as favourable as possible for the gods.

In Norse mythology, the future was thought to be somewhat
fluid and capable of being altered by actions in the present.

Odin (OH-din): the All-Father, chief god in the Norse
pantheon.

Ragnarök (RAGG-na-rock): the Final Battle, where the Aesir
and their allies would battle with monsters and Jotuns. It
would be the end of the world, though it was written a new
green world would emerge. Odin was always attempting
to make things come out better in the battle, to gain an
advantage over the giants and monsters the heroes and gods of
Asgard would be fighting.

reðri (REH-three): Old Norse slang for penis.

seithkona (Sayth-KONA-ah): practitioners of *seithr*, almost
always women. They were valued and often wealthy.

seithr (SAY-th-urr): a kind of Norse magic often associated with weaving. It incorporates a dimension of spirituality and life force and was regarded with great respect.

Sigrene (Sig-GREEN): the story's protagonist, whose mother was the goddess Freyja. She had four fathers, dwarrow kings: Dvalinn, Alfrik, Berling, and Grer. Sigrene was the name given to the protagonist at Urd's Well after she had surrendered her previous names to the Norns, who had snipped them out of the weaving on the World Loom. Her given name had been Esja, though it was seldom used. Previous to going to Urd's Well, the protagonist had been nicknamed Sparrow.

skeið (Skeh): a gait unique to Icelandic horses, a flying pace that requires a horse to perform a lateral gait where both legs on one side of the horse simultaneously touch the ground. Performed at speed, there are points at which no hooves will be in contact with the ground.

Sleipnir (SLAY-p-neer): Odin's horse in Norse mythology. Sleipnir was called "eight-legged" by bards. Painters who have taken this literally failed to take into account the tradition of figurative language, including kennings; for example, "flame-farewelled" for an implicitly honourable death. Sleipnir's parents were the god Loki and a giant's horse. He was the first skyhorse.

Sessrúmnir (SESS-room-near): Freyja's hall.

skyhorses: paintings of Valkyries show them mounted on horses, hovering above the battlefields. The horses have no wings. In this adaptation of mythology, skyhorses step the air currents between the Realms. The skyhorses enable the gods to travel around the World Tree, Yggdrasil.

spindle (SPIN-del): a round stick with tapered ends used to form and twist the yarn in hand spinning. The word *wand* comes from this. The Norse word for this was *seiostafr*.

Telerion (TEL-ear-EE-on): a gold and amber cuff crafted by Sigrene's fathers and given to her as a gift. It matched Freyja's fabled necklace Brísingamen.

Thor (TH-ore): the Norse god of thunder.

thrall (TH-rall): a servant/slave.

Tyr (TEA-rrh): warlord of the Aesir. Of all the gods, he was the one who could be counted on to uphold the law. He was a god to be relied on, not a cheat like some of the others.

Valhalla (Val-HA-la): Odin's hall.

Valkyrie (VAL-keer-ee-ah): shield-maidens of Norse mythology, often half gods. Their job was to observe human battles and pluck especially distinguished warriors to live again in the halls of Freyja and Odin. Valkyries were distinguished fighters themselves.

Vanaheim (VAN-ah-hi-mm): a realm where a race of gods older than the Aesir lived. The Vanir had a reputation in Asgard for being secretive.

wergild (WEAR-gild): blood money. Reparations paid by a killer to a victim's family to avoid a blood feud and killings that might otherwise go on for generations.

Yggdrasil (IGG-dra-zeel): the World Tree in Norse mythology. It holds up the Nine Realms.

Ymir (YIM-meer): was the first being, a Frost Giant, formed when ice from Niflheim and flames from Muspelheim crept toward one another until they met in Ginnungagap. He was killed by Odin and his brothers, who constructed the world from Ymir's corpse. They made the sky from his skull.

For pointers on Old Norse pronunnciation, I am grateful to Dr. Jackson CRawford, Old Norse specialist currently at the University of Colarado as a Resident Scholar. Any errors are mine.

I've been reading about Norse myths since I was eight. Here are a few books for those interested in further exploration.

Byock, Jesse L., *The Prose Edda: Norse Mythology*, Penguin 2005

Crawford, Jackson, *The Poetic Edda*, Hackett Publishing Company, 2015

Crawford, Jackson, *Saga of the Volsungs*, Hackett Publishing Company, 2017

Larrington, Carolyn, *The Norse Myths: A Guide to Viking and Scandinavian Gods and Heroes*, Thames and Hudson, 2017

Larrington, Carolyn, *The Poetic Edda*, Oxford University Press, 2019

Larrington, C., J. Quinn and B. Schorn,eds., *A Handbook to Eddic Poetry: Myths and Legends of Ancient Scandinavia*, Cambridge University Press, 2016

ENDNOTES

1 Valuable dwarrow-work was always named.

2 In the Norse, Asgard and Midgard end with "gard," the word for garden. The other realms names end in "heim" the word for home. The supposition is the inhabitants of the higher realms, Alfheim and Vanaheim, possess a different relationship to nature, which is allowed to develop in much wilder fashion than in the garden worlds.

3 The Norns' blessing was an invocation that Sigrene could remember and continue to use:

Light before me
Light behind me
Light above me
Light beneath me
Light to my left hand
Light to my right hand

4 With the bolded text, Sigrene is invoking *seithr*.

5 According to the prophecies, until Ragnarök, Niddhogg was supposed to be confined to a hole in the ground where she gnawed the root of the World Tree. It was a sign that the Last Battle was very close when she flew free.

6 The captain of the Valkyries doesn't use Anfinn's name because she doesn't want to call the dead man back as an angry ghost.

7 Brendan's remark is taken from a prayer that came to be called St Patrick's Breastplate, a slightly different rendering of the line "Christ in the mouth of friend and stranger."

8 The actual Realms that make up Norse mythology are fluid, depending on what texts one is reading. Where the Realms are located and who lives there is debated in the literature. While the Realms are commonly referred to as "the Nine Realms" there are actually more like ten. It's one of the interesting features of Norse mythology that characters move around and sometimes one well-known individual seems to break into two with similar names but different functions. Legends shift into stories that splinter but seem very similar, and locales are identified with great authority by the Eddas in different ways. Scholars feel that this may be a result of the literature shifting and being re-interpreted over the course of hundreds of years. Is Freyja really the same character as Frigg? How old is the saga or Edda that you're reading? Was it reinterpreted by a later writer?

McGill University, in a post on Wikipedia, makes the interesting point that Norse mythology is not easily divided into the duality of good guys and bad guys. Jotuns, humans, elves, Aesir, Vanir are all capable of making nuanced decisions. According to this reference, the only truly "evil" class of being are the fire giants, and they are more of an elemental force than beings making moral choices.

Please understand that that the way I've come to understand the Realms is a personal interpretation.

DISCUSSION QUESTIONS

Although Sigrene is consistently unable to see her own strengths, what do you notice about her character and actions that indicates she is more than a downtrodden victim? Do you see parallels in some women's lives today?

Does Freyja's attitude toward her daughter change over the course of the story? What is the final sign touched on toward the end that might show Freyja's feelings?

Why do you think that Sigrene forgets what's woven in the World Loom after she leaves Urd's Well? She sees how she might be able to change a few threads to save Sleipnir's life and then that knowledge evaporates until she's sitting opposite Odin in his hall, Valhalla. She says at that point, "Is there a favour I might do for you, wisest of gods?" What comes back to her at this point?

As Sigrene rides Bright-mane down to the lowest level of Hel, what brings on her vision of a sunlit world where there is no word for vengeance?

How fair is the bargain that Sigrene makes with Odin? After all, she doesn't know what she's actually agreeing to.

What do the skyhorses represent to Sigrene? What do you see her doing that indicates this?

Do you think that Sigrene fights with the Aesir and their allies in the Final Battle? She would need to be close enough to see Odin fall. Yet she's not the strongest of fighters and if she gets killed, she wouldn't be able to save the Sleipnir and the mares in foal.

Why does Sigrene bring Addý with her into the new green world?

ACKNOWLEDGEMENTS

Thanks to the Árni Magnússon Institute for Icelandic Studies who granted me a residency in Reykjavik to do research for this book.

My sincere appreciation goes out to Kwantlen Polytechnic University, where I taught for fifteen years. Kwantlen awarded me a travel grant and a research grant for these poems. The Woodcock Foundation also gave me a grant to complete this book for which I am very grateful.

Huge thanks to Nicola MacWilliam and Shannon Bailey who helped me both to workshop and to keep the faith. Joy Thierry Llewellyn, your insightful comments saved the day!

Leslie Munro assisted me with bending my brain around weaving: many thanks for your info!

Any mistakes I may have made are mine.

Those who are familiar with Norse mythology will recognize that Sigrene, Krista, Addý, Buri, haunts, fog-spiders, and the cuff Telerion belong to the Realm of imagination. Everything else is according to the sagas.

Credit: Ingrid Paulsen

Zoë Landale has published ten books, mainly poetry. She's also edited two books, and her work appears in around fifty anthologies. Her writing has won significant awards in three genres, including first in the Stony Brook University Short Fiction competition, National Magazine Gold for memoir, and first in the CBC Literary Competition for poetry.

She taught for fifteen years as a faculty member in the Creative Writing Department at Kwantlen Polytechnic University in Vancouver, British Columbia.

Landale lives on Pender Island, one of BC's southern Gulf islands. Connect with her at: magicmonday.substack.com